T0107449

Deep in
in
Serenity

Deep in
in
Serenity

DP Jones

DEEP IN SERENITY

Copyright © 2017 DP Jones.

All rights reserved. No part of this book may be used or reproduced by any means, graphic, electronic, or mechanical, including photocopying, recording, taping or by any information storage retrieval system without the written permission of the author except in the case of brief quotations embodied in critical articles and reviews.

iUniverse books may be ordered through booksellers or by contacting:

iUniverse
1663 Liberty Drive
Bloomington, IN 47403
www.iuniverse.com
1-800-Authors (1-800-288-4677)

Because of the dynamic nature of the Internet, any web addresses or links contained in this book may have changed since publication and may no longer be valid. The views expressed in this work are solely those of the author and do not necessarily reflect the views of the publisher, and the publisher hereby disclaims any responsibility for them.

Any people depicted in stock imagery provided by Thinkstock are models, and such images are being used for illustrative purposes only. Certain stock imagery © Thinkstock.

ISBN: 978-1-5320-3088-8 (sc)
ISBN: 978-1-5320-3089-5 (e)

Print information available on the last page.

iUniverse rev. date: 08/02/2018

This could possibly be a true story, names could've been changed
Never Assume Unless you know the FACTS
If you don't know, now you know
So here it is, my story
LIVE IN THE MOMENT
Enjoy Life
1LovE

GONE

Dawayne pulled up to the apartment complex,

he saw the light in his living room illuminating. His heart thumped loud, he could hear it in his ear beating like a drum. The feeling was overwhelming, he didn't know whether to stay in the car or run up the stairs. He got out his car, and took his time up the flights of stairs. He slowly opened the door, hoping he would surprise whoever was lurking in his apartment. His heart was in his throat, it was hard to breath. Was this really happening, was this going to be the day. Dawayne slowly stepped into his apartment, he was looking for that familiar scent. He searched in every room, nothing, not a fucking thing. He missed her, he knew that feeling. The feeling of not being complete, not being whole. "Where are you, he whispered," he knew she was nowhere near. Dawayne went to his bathroom, her red towel was still there folded and placed ever so neatly. He took it into his hands and inhaled, the smell was gone. Her scent had vanished, slowly like the water in a puddle evaporating into the air. He remembered when Serenity would take a shower, with the door open and he could smell that scent. That scent that was only her, which scent had lasted a little over a month. Until tonight, it was gone, the only thing that made him know it was all real, that he was not living a lie, that this was not all a dream. All he had left was the memories of that MOMENT they shared. All shared and given items were placed carefully, and neatly packed into the B.O.M. Only the two of them knew what secrets were placed inside the Box of Memories. They had put every gift, every letter, every moment they shared into that box. Sealed into with tape, so it could be waterproof, and could not be confused for anything other than a big ass box. With orange and black duct tape, in the strangest design made with the tape. They made a vow that, Dawayne would take the box, where ever he went. They would not open it up, or dispose of it, unless both of them were there in the flesh.

The day Serenity left was the worst day of his life, he felt sick, and in some weird way. He thought that she wouldn't leave, he had fought for her, the way every woman wants to be fought for. All twelve rounds, sweat, blood, tears, and still didn't bring home the win. How he didn't want her to leave, the only thing he didn't do is hang on to her leg as she left. How could something so right, something that felt so real, the missing piece of his life just up and left. Dawayne cried that night like a lil bitch and held on to what memories of Serenity he had left. Let's get you on track to how and when this all began. We would have to go back to the year 2015, this is when it all started.

SERENITY

It was a cool spring day, and Dawayne was cooking in the mess hall when she walked into. Her caramel skin, and long legs caught his eye. She had been coming in everyday to eat and each time he had this urge that he could not resist. She had been giving him the FUCK ME eyes for quite some time, but today was going to be different. For some reason it was going to be different, the energy was overwhelming, and you can't stop an energy like that. She had got his attention and handed him a small paper box, and inside that box was something that would change his life forever. The note said," I can't help myself I am attracted to older man, and I think I have a thing for you." Dawayne was in shock, he didn't know if this was a joke or some dare the other students had put her up to. So he replied back, "If that's how you feel than make the first leap." He carefully placed it back into the paper box, and waited for her to pass by him again. His nerves were getting the best of him, should he be doing this, could he get in trouble. He said, "fuck it," and just went with the flow. She passed by and he got her attention, he smoothly passed the paper box into her hand. Trying not to be seen by any other staff, or students in the mess hall. This feeling Dawayne felt was so right and a so taboo in the same way. That night when he went home, all he could think about was her, her golden caramel skin, and those long FUCKING legs, GOD those legs. He couldn't sleep that night, all he could think about was the possibilities, and outcomes. Dawayne's imagination got the best of him sometimes, when it comes to thinking of the worst case scenario. He got about three hours of sleep that night, but when he woke up he was rejuvenated, he felt new. There was his best friend paranoia, paranoia if anything would be the death of him one day if he didn't get a hold his life. That day he left his apartment with purpose, with an idea. He was going to write a note with 6 letters, which meant something, she would never get it. He laughed about how he was going to have her thinking what those 6 letters meant on that paper. ICMYDCT, was what was written on small page ripped from his small note pad. In his head he was thinking of the possibilities with those letters, she came in that day for dinner. Once again looking like a Nubian Queen from near the equator, long beautiful legs, caramel skin, and her eyes.

Her eyes seemed different, the color they were green, a tinge of green, interesting he thought. In that moment he saw a vision, of her and him, the say the eyes are the window to the soul. She was sitting with her friend, he gave her the note in a napkin, and she opened it. Looked at the letters and immediately asked, "Does that say I Can Make Your Dreams Come True?" FUCK he thought, how in the fuck could she get that so quick. He tried to pull it off cool, but when she made eye contact with him he could not lie. He didn't even have to say a word, she knew that's what it meant. How could this be, he thought it would at least take her a day to have the answer. Before she left she placed the napkin into his apron, he went into the bathroom to read what she had wrote. Holy Bobby Brown, he was freaking out, paranoia was lurking behind the shadows of his thoughts. He double checked the door, to make sure it was locked. Then he slowly opened up the napkin, the paper read" ICMYDCT2." What the fuck was happening, was this real, he even bit his lip, and to feel the pain he didn't realize he bite so hard. He could taste the iron in his mouth, the taste of blood. So real, there is no way this was a dream, reality hit and the blood in his veins began to glow bright blue from under his skin.

Days went by, and the continuation of passing of notes did as well. Then there was that evening that he took the leap. Dawayne was getting ready to work the dinner shift that night and he felt like he could take the world on in a zombie apocalypse on his own, he had this built up courage. The mess hall had been packed that night, there must have been something popping off later on campus. He had tried to be as patient as possible, but then all of a sudden his nerves started getting the best of him. The mess hall, began to empty, as the students were in a rush to get there food and start their Friday night.

There was about five students in the mess hall, and then she came walking in. She was wearing a white dress, and it showed off those FUCKING legs. He was beginning to think that she may have had other plans. She came in and got a sprite, and not a lot of food. She sat down, as she sat down it seemed as if the world had been put in slow motion. Yet Dawayne had forgot to blink the whole time she came in to get her meal.

By the time he blinked the mess hall was empty and she was the only one there. Dawayne's supervisor was in the back counting the till. So he thought this would be the only chance he got, as he moved from behind the expo station she was gone.

She was fucking GONE, but he noticed her tray was still at the table. The lavatory door was closed, so she must be in there." Now is the time," he thought to himself. The door opened and he slowly stepped in the way, using his body to gently guide her back into the room. He grabbed the back of her neck with one hand and grabbed a handful of her natural hair. Once his hands were on her body there was a spark of static between them. When he placed his lips on to her lips it had created a small shock, as they both looked into the others eyes they saw a glow. A glowing blue in her eyes, and burning red in his eyes. When they kissed "Holy Bobby Brown," when they kissed you would have thought they were lovers reunited. That moment lasted about 3 minutes, and when he let go and pulled back. He could feel her energy wanting more, pulling him close. So he went with the flow, he whispered in her ear Serenity. That was the first time he had said her name, she had a control over him, the way a snake charmer has over a King Cobra. He felt free, felt like this moment was going to last forever. Too bad for the both of them, he had totally forgot that his ass was at work. "SHIT," he whispered where the hell did you just take me? She then pulled him into her by his chef coat, kissed him like she would never see him again. Whispering, "I told you I Can Make Your Dreams Come True 2," she walked passed him got her tray and left the mess hall. Dawayne was paralyzed from the lips down, he could still feel that warmth that energy the shock left on his lips. He turned around and walked straight into his supervisor. "What the fuck are you doing Dawayne," he asked. He didn't know how long his boss had been standing there, but he couldn't muster a word. "Are the lavatories clean, and area secure?" his boss asked. Yea yea, yup yup, k k, the words that came from his mouth even surprised him. He was lucky his boss didn't see him do what, he think he just had done.

Did it really happen, there is no way the Dawyne he knew would ever do such a foolish thing. Or was it foolish? That night as he left the mess hall, his head was replaying that moment in the lavatory. He pulled his car keys out his pocked and dropped them, not once 4 fucking times. Was that kiss that hypnotizing he couldn't even handle his damn keys? He opened the door, and sat in the driver seat for a second, took a deep breath and went for the ignition. Dropping his keys again, "What the fuck," he said to himself, you got this it's not that hard just put the key in the ignition. Dropped once more, "Fuck it," he cursed under his breath and put the key in the ignition and started his car.

He pulled out of the parking lot and headed to his crib. He had the music blasting and was sing the lyrics to "Good Thing, "by Nick Jonas and Sage the Gemini. Dawayne was singing those lyrics like he had written that song." Isn't nothing but dangerous, why can't it be what it is," soon as he sang that part he saw the flashing lights. "Oh shit," he thought he needed to get out the way for the cop. The cop continued to follow behind him, what the fuck was this cop's problem. Then he looked at the speedometer, and noticed he was cruising, the cop was for him. He turned the music down and pulled over, "how fast was I driving," he asked himself. Dawayne waited for the cop to get out his BMW, as the cop walked closer to Dawayne he began to think. Yet what came out of his mouth when the officer, asked him why he got pulled over," you were doing 75 in a 45 "He said." I just had the most amazing expertise a men could ever have." The cop gave him a look, license and registration sir." Dawayne got in his center consul and grabbed his registration. Did that really come out of his mouth, I just had the most amazing experience a man could have. Who says shit like that, apparently him. The cop went back to his beamer and did whatever it is cops do before the give you a ticket. The cop got out of the beamer and walked back in his direction. Handing him his license and registration back. He looked at Dawayne and laughed, "You're in love son, and I can see the fire burning in your eyes." "I'm not going to give you a ticket this time, because I've been in your shoes son just slow down." The cop turned and hopped in his car, "What the fuck just happened, AGAIN?" He was grateful, and on cloud nine, he drove home thinking of that kiss, and all the letters they had been writing to each other. He made it home after making sure he followed the speed limit. He thought what the chances not getting a ticket are, he had been pulled over numerous times. Throwing tickets like parades throw candy at kids. Dawayne was not a lucky person, like he had been luck in his past. This was a whole new thing, getting pulled over and not getting a ticket. Did that spark between him and Serenity break the curse of bad luck? All that was on his mind was that kiss, he walked up the flights of stairs to his apartment and unlocked his door. Kicked his shoes off, and headed for the room. Got undressed, hooked his phone to his beats pill and bumped smooth r&b off his soundcloud. That had to been the longest shower he had ever taken in his life, and no he wasn't playing wack a mole.

He was just enjoying the scorching pellets of liquid hit his body, until the water heater ran out of hot water. He had been in the shower for longer than an hour, he turned off the water and opened the curtain. Grabbed for his towel, couldn't see it the steam had been thick, and it didn't help he showered in the dark. He didn't know why, just something he did, he threw his towel on the bed and feel onto his bed. He woke up to a sound, a very familiar sound. It was his phone, someone was calling him, and he looked at his phone. It was his alarm it was 8:24, "Shit, Fuck, Fuck," he screamed he had slept through his alarm. The worst part is he didn't even have any clothes on, he was still buck ass naked. He hadn't even crawled under his comforter, he was still on his neatly made bed, and towel was wrapped around his leg. A few months passed by and the flow of electricity between Dawayne and Serenity continued to spark. The two were playing the game sneak and don't tell, the would sneak kisses in whenever they could. He would take a handful of that ass whenever he could as she would sometimes, pass by slowly. Intentionally slowly rubbing her body against his when she would pass him.

THE OFFICE

The night in the mess hall was busy, Dawayne's supervisor had to leave due to a family situation. That had left Dawayne in charge, he was now the go to guy if there was any problems. As usual Serenity came in later on into dinner, it was more packed when they opened and there were more eyes watching. So a lil later after dinner started was always the best time to come in. Her friend Wynter was right behind her, sometime she would show up with Serenity, and sometimes she wouldn't. Wynter was Serenity's best friend. Wynter had mahogany skin, and that beautiful natural black woman hair. There are many black women that use extensions and weave, not Wynter. She was an all-natural kind of woman. Two beautiful confident black women, just enjoying themselves with some conversation and food. Dawayne was almost done with lock up, and the rest of the staff was on their way out the door. He wasn't sure if Serenity was still there, he did se Wynter leave the mess hall. So Dawayne thought that the area was secure, and he turned off the lights to the area. As he was heading to the back of the house, he heard a door open. It was Serenity, she had snuck her way into the back without him knowing. He walked towards her, and cornered her in the women's lavatory. The energy in the bathroom began to glow, and pulsate. Serenity played the innocent victim as he grabbed her. The sexual creature that was festering inside of him couldn't be held back any longer. He unbuttoned her shorts, and slowly pulled them down her legs. To his surprise, she had been wearing no panties. He put his hands on her body, with each touch of his fingertips should could feel surges of energy. Dawayne's fingers found their way to her SWEETNESS, Serenity took a deep breath. As if with each touch of his fingers, he was taken the air from her lungs. With each exhale, she could feel her body wanting more. He slid his middle finger into the folds of her SWEETNESS, it was so wet, so fucking wet. He wanted to taste it, he wanted to know what she tasted like. He explored the inner walls of her SWEETNESS, and pulled his finger out. He couldn't resist, he put his finger to his mouth. Sucking his fingers he tasted her for the first time, so sweet, everything you would expect and more. Serenity gave him a look, like WTF, he slid his fingers along the outline of her frame.

As he fingers slowly passed her thigh, and got closer to the SWEETNESSS, he went for it. He placed his hand right on the spot. He rubbed it slowly, up and down. Polishing her SWEETNESS, with her own nectar. He took his finger again to his mouth, and as Serenity looked him in the eye. He placed two fingers on the fullest part of her bottom lip. She opened her mouth and sucked his fingers, sucked to point that she had even gagged herself with his finger. Serenity began to work on his belt. He could tell she was frustrated, he did have a pretty tricky belt on. In the back of his mind the monster paranoia was trying to get the best of him, she looked into his eyes and said," You have easy eyes." Soon as she said that, his belt became unlatched and his erection flopped out. Before he knew it he was almost inside her, and he thought protection. He grabbed the golden package he had in his work bag. Why did he even have a condom in his back pack, ok he knew what. Because of Serenity she had been telling him he needs to LITM. Live in the moment, you never know when shit is going down. He came back with it on, and his dick hard as titanium, "be gentle", she whispered. He looked into her eyes and with that look Serenity knew that he would take care of her, never hurt her, and only do what it takes to please her. Serenity hiked up one leg on the counter top in the lavatory, holy Bobby Brown her SWEETNESS was so wetttt. He took his time getting to know her walls, they were tight and he didn't want to hurt her. She arched her back as he went in deeper and deeper, he wanted to tease her. All those moments that she told him after the fact, that he could a, should a, would a. He pulled the shaft of his muscle all most completely out, just leaving the head. He slowly pulled in and out of her SWEETNESS. Causing Serenity to feel something she had never got the privilege to feel. That nirvana, he flipped her over and had her ass on the counter. His muscle had been inside the walls, she was convulsing, and her legs were shacking. Serenity had come, the feeling that came over her was nothing that she had ever experienced in her life. Dawayne then asked, "You ready for some nigga shit." As he asked that Dawayne placed his arms under her thighs, cuffing her round plump ass. In the same motion before she knew it they were straight fucking.

Her feet were no longer on the floor or holding anything. He had his muscle inside her and she wrapped her arms around his neck, holding on for dear life. While Serenity was full airborne getting the walls of her SWEETNESS pounded. Dawayne decided to take it from the lavatory to the Chef's office. He was smooth with the transition, not losing his momentum, and the rhythm moving to the office. That's when he decided to put his game on another level. Smooth as Floyd Money Mayweather, he grabbed tight behind her ass, and lifted up. Serenity looked down and realized she was sitting on his shoulders. He was something else, what the fuck was she doing on his shoulders. How the fuck was he able to savor, and taste all of what she had in between them long, slender legs mid-flight. She felt her body opening up to the possibilities, she bent her wrist and placed her hands flat on the ceiling. She was going to enjoy this, every tongue flick, every trace, every pulse. He had her on his shoulders, her shirt was half way off. He slid the length of his tongue inside the folds of her SWEETNESS, his tongue shifted right then left, then circled, than zig zagged. Serenity felt this blast of warm arm on her body, sweat was glistening from her body. It smelt so sweet, looked so good, Dawayne then took his face from her SWEETNESS, moving his head up to meet her stomach. He began to lick, on her stomach, taking each bead of sweat that was present on your body. Placing them on the tip of his tongue, and ending each suckle with a gentle kiss. Dawayne looked at Serenity, the look of defeat is in her eyes. He gently releases the grasp he has on her legs, and her feet finally touch ground. She thought that her feet would never touch the ground again, that is the level of highness she was on. Dawayne looked at the clock, 45 minutes had passed by. He should be on his way home by now, but this was what living in the moment meant. He sat down on the office chair, muscle still erect. With that Serenity took her time straddling him. Their bodies were clammy from the sweat and the sexual energy they shared. He wrapped his arms around her, and she kissed him. She grabbed the shaft of his muscle and guided it to her SWEETNESS. It was so wet, so warm, and the walls were tight as fuck. Serenity straddled that dick, moved her hips she was giving him a ride to remember for the way home.

She pulled him in closer, wanting all of him. The blood was rushing so fast through his muscle, Serenity could actually feel the blood flow travel through each artery, each vessel. With that his muscle felt empowering, he had been enjoying the moment. He had given her a lil taste of what he could do, and she was riding him. Riding him as if he were the bull, and she was the rider. Dawayne pulled Serenity in close and whispered in her ear, "I love you. " What the fuck you just said, he thought to himself. " He had been holding back those words for some time, he was trying not to use them in a scenario such as this. He wanted it to be special when he said it, this moment was special, but yeah there was a butt. Serenity let her grip loose around his neck, and just have him a lil look. He knew what that look was, she heard him say, I love you. He did mean it, just didn't want to be that guy. The guy that uses the word love to get what he wants. This was far from that LOVE, what he felt was sincere, and true. He had not felt like this in years, maybe it was the danger of getting caught, maybe it was the adrenaline. All he knew in that moment, was that he wanted to spend the rest of his life with her. Crazy as it may have sounded, the same idea was floating around in Serenity's head as well.

TABLE ETIQUETTE

Table Etiquette, you may wonder why this chapter is named table etiquette. Well the definition of table etiquette is defined as the following. Table manners are the rules of etiquette used while eating, which may also include the appropriate use of utensils.

Dawayne had and has horrible table etiquette, you may be asking yourself why he has such horrible table etiquette. Let's not go too far ahead of ourselves, a few days passed as the sexual tension between Serenity and Dawayne pulsed. Dawayne's supervisor had went on vacation and he was in charge for the next couple weeks. This was his chance to let out his inner creature. The days had all jumbled together, from the last time they had shared a moment. He wanted to try something crazy, something that would be completely taboo. The night started innocent and it was just another ordinary meal, the population came in to eat and get the fuck out. Shit it was Friday night and they were playing a movie in the lounge, and if you didn't get your spot early. Your ass would end up having to sit on the floor. Serenity came in early and she was with her friend Wynter. They got their food and went across the mess hall to where they were hidden. Dawayne saw them come in, as he and Serenity shared glances at each other. He saw that mystical look in her eye, and she saw something brewing in him. She had a feeling that something was about to happen, like she could always feel his energy that he gave off. Mostly and mainly sexual but there was something different in the energy that he was giving off. The mess hall became just a few stragglers, and Serenity and Wynter were up still chillin in the same spot. "Time to go ladies," Dawayne said as he had that look in his eye, for Serenity to stay back. Wynter wasn't stupid, she knew what was going on, how you could not get engulfed with that energy the two had between them. Wynter knew what was going on between them before Serenity knew it was something. That's one thing about Wynter, when it comes to being a real and down ride or die friend. Wynter was that BITCH, that kind of friend that would be down for you know matter what. That was Wynter, as she walked out the mess hall leaving her bestie. She said," you two don't do anything that I wouldn't do," and she had the biggest grin on her face. She left laughing and Dawayne locked up behind her, and that's when Serenity ran across the mess hall. As if she were trying to hide from him, she ended up cornering herself between two tables

He pushed her up into the table to her right, he grabbed her by the hips. Sitting her on top of the table, he pulled her leggings off. As if they were a present and he was a lil boy opening up his gift. She had a pink and black lace thong on underneath, he started to his and suck on her hips.

Moving to her side, and moving his tongue on her like he was blind and his tongue was his walking stick. Dawayne bit down on the side of Serenity's thong, and pulled it down with his teeth. As Serenity arched her back, her legs began to wrap around his neck. He took the side of his tongue and slid it down the length of her long slender leg. His tongue skating along the walls of her SWEETNESS, like a figure skater. He would flick his tongue against the neatly so hidden clit, she was wett and sweet, so FUCKING sweet. Serenity had forgotten she was on the table, she was sliding off the table onto his shoulders. Serenity mind was starting to come back, she thought how many people would eat off this table after this. Dawayne took all of her SWEETNESS into his mouth. Massaging it with his lower lip, while flicking his tongue at the same time. Serenity said," I hope you like your dessert." He replied with more stimulation to the walls of her SWEETNESS, he could feel her heart beat in each fold. Serenity had a tingle in her body, it started from her toes, and slowly moved up her leg. The electric current of sexual energy had taken over her body, the red sexual energy from him was slowly colliding with the electric blue surges of energy Serenity had. Her body erupted, and she lost all control of her body and mind. He had taken her to a place they would soon call ELECUPHORIA. These taboo and very sexual sessions continued for many days. One night while Dawayne was closing and everybody was gone, Serenity sneaked her way into the back of the kitchen. Dawayne was doing his normal checks and when he came back to the front she was there. Wearing nothing but his chef coat, he had never seen a chef coat look so fucking sexy in his life. She said to him in the sexiest voice," If you want your coat back you're going to have to take it off me." He walked over to her slowly, his legs were like jello. He couldn't believe she was standing there in only a chef coat. He pulled her in by the hips and said," This is the sexiest things I've ever seen."

With that he began kissing and sucking on her neck, he moved his fingers over the buttons of the chef coat. His fingers had turned into soft sticks of butter, he was having some complications unbuttoning this coat, and he had been doing it for years. In his mind he was telling himself it's just a fucking button how hard can it be, apparently it was that difficult. Serenity looked into his eyes, with just that action, just that since of energy she carried. Dawayne was able to calm the fuck down and say, "Fuck you paranoia."

He got into the flow of unbuttoning the coat, the coat fell to the ground, and her dark brown nipples were erect. The moment the coat fell to the ground Serenity got the chills, there was something about Dawayne. Something that brought her to piece and caused her body and mind to lose control. The electric sexual energy that was pinned up inside him would pulsate through her every time he touched her. He hoisted her onto the prep table and started sucking on her erect nipples. Holding on to the middle of her back, with his dominate hand. Running his fingers with his left hand down the side of her face, to her neck to her lips. His only purpose in this moment was to get her to come and scream it out. Dawayne guided her onto her back, and placed his lips on her stomach. She quivered, as the red sexual energy from him was exploring all the nerve endings of her body. His mouth moved closer to her SWEETNESS, and as his tongue landed on a wet and so so sweet and juicy fold. Serenity forgot to breathe, his tongue was oh so mystical. The way he moved his tongue was, as if he had gotten a Degree in Contemporary Dance of the Tongue. He pulled the condom out of his pocket, slid it on with ease. He enjoyed teasing the walls of her SWEETNESS, with just the head. He would take just the tip and slide it up and down the moist folds. He would insert just a lil bit, and then he would continue going back to the outer walls. Only when she would say, "You're a tease." He would fill her with his muscle, but even then he wouldn't give her the whole thing. You just can't give it all, you have to be slow and steady and patient. Sex to Dawayne wasn't something to take lightly, it was an art it was beautiful. When you have a canvas laying there in front of you naked and wanting it. Your tongue, your muscle, your fingers become the paint brush, and you get to create a masterpiece.

Serenity couldn't take the teasing anymore, she grabbed his ass and pulled him in. Taking all of his muscle, she let out a loud moan, that moan came from her inner sexual creature. We all have that creature inside of us, some black out when it takes over. Some have been able to train, and condition that creature. So when it comes you can handle it and take the sexual energy and sexual act to a LEVEL that only few have come in contact with. Dawayne felt her walls tighten around his muscle, he was deep in the SWEETNESS. Serenity was still gripping onto his ass, holding him deep inside her. To the point that her nails were digging into the flesh of his ass. He didn't mind that just gave him more fuel, to beat the pussy up.

He knew what she was feeling was good, and that she wanted more. Not a sample, not a test drive, she wanted to take it home and ride it till it feel off. Till he was sore, couldn't withstand that feeling of her walls wrapped so tightly around his muscle. They stayed in that one position of her holding him inside her deep, for what seemed like an hour. He had not even put in the effort to attempt a full stroke, he was at peace with where his muscle was. It was hard as titanium, and the blood running through his muscles caused waves of energy to tap dance on the inner folds of her SWEETNESS. He never kept his hands still, they moved across her body touching every inch of her beautiful caramel body.

She pulled him in even more, and he could tell by the look in her eye that she was full, the transportation to ELECUPHORIA had been complete. As she pulled him in to the edge of her walls, he grabbed her by the neck and kissed her. The passion that was put into this kiss, the energy was enough to light up the deepest and darkest caves on the planet. His sexual creature had been present, had been lurking in the allies of his body. His creature wanted to devour her SWEETNESS, swell her walls to the point it was untouchable. The slightest breath, or cross wind would cause her body to go into a sexual coma. He pulled away from her and began his stoke, his stroke had purpose, the definition of his muscle each inch was felt in her inner walls. ELECUPHORIA was an amazing place, and only with him it could be reached. His strokes where long and slow, making sure Serenity felt every inch.

Every surge of sexual energy he had. Her ass left the table and her legs found there place on his chest, with her toes in the air. So tight so juicy, so wet, her SWEETNESS was the best he had ever had. He was the best she had ever had, his sex game was on point. On a new level, unable to put in words or describe, it was just on that LEVEL. Serenity wanted more she pushed him away, and turned around and bent over the prep table. She hiked one leg up on the table, grabbed his muscle and guided it to her SWEETNESS. It slid in with ease, she was wet, and he could see her creamy nectar holding on to her folds. She was high enough, there was no need to squat or get on his tippy toes. That was the advantage with having sexual sessions with someone close to same height, she was tall and he was tall. FUCK those legs, Holy Bobby Brown those legs, he wish he could be like" Honey We Shrunk the Kids." Just be small enough to explore every inch, every fold, of her body.

Being that small he could take a month long journey to know her body, to explore. She was bouncing her SWEETNESS on his muscle, grinding, he put his hands on her back. It was glistening from the sweat, beads of sweat were slowly finding the way to her lower back. He moved his lips toward her neck, sucking and licking. He even took the glistening beads of sweat trickling down her back onto the tip of his tongue. Her body quivered with electricity, Dawayne was a FUCKING magician with the way he had control of her, she was thinking. The way he would move his energy over her body, and cause her body to engulf it. Dawayne eyes moved towards the clock on the wall, 11:45 damn he should of been out Time had stood still once again, it was way past the time he should've been out an hour and 45 minutes ago. SHIT, FUCK, SHIT, Serenity yelled, she was way past curfew and she would have to sneak her way back to her dormitory. He sneaked her out the back, trying not to be seen or heard. No need for anyone to catch them know, as Serenity walked around the corner she ran into her friend Ebony. "Where the fuck you been girl, I was bout ready to hit the fire alarm." "I've looked everywhere for you and nobody knew where you were, have a nigga straight worried about your black ass."

Serenity didn't answer she just kept walking, as her friend was asking where she had been for the last 45 minutes. They walked around the campus for a while, Serenity was still coming down from the adrenaline, and body high. It wasn't even a few days later, before Serenity found herself on the pastry table. She had come in late like she had been doing the past couple weeks, and had purpose. The hunger for the feeling that she had when she was with Dawayne. He made her happy, made her laugh, and most important appreciated her and all her that molecules that made her into what was the flesh she was. Soon she was on the table and he was flicking his tongue on the outside of her SWEETNESS. His tongue carefully gliding between her folds. She could feel this built up pressure inside her, like she had to pee. The sensation was to intense Serenity quickly rolled off the table and ran to the pantry. Dawayne slowly walked to the pantry, he saw her there trying to hide behind some racks. He had her cornered, he lifted up her shirt and went for her nipples. Serenity moved his face out the way with her hand. That's when Dawayne grabbed both her hands with his right and pulled them over her head. Holding on to her as if he was a restraint, she moaned and bit her lip.

He went back to her nipple, sucking with more intensity. Serenity moaned, and moved her body to the rhythm of their heart beats. He slid his other hand down the side of her face, taking his time. With each swoop of his finger, she got the chills. He moved along the veins of her neck, moving to the definition of her collarbone. He then moved down the side of her ribs, she gasped for air as her body quivered. His finger glided along her hip bone, tiptoeing over her pelvis. Gliding back up to her navel, and slowly making a trail up the middle of her body between her breasts. Circling her areola, his finger went to his mouth. Leaving some wetness on the tips of his finger, blowing on it. To cool it, so he could trace her areola and cause her nipple to become more erect. He sucked on her nipple, slightly nibbling, pulling, and biting on them. Giving both breast and nipple the same amount of attention. Dawayne made sure both received the proper amount of attention, and stimulation.

"Wait," Serenity gasped, she was trying to control the situation. "Stop," Dawayne hesitated but then pulled away. Serenity moved her hands towards his belt, slowly working the belt free. She unbuttoned his pants, pulled the zipper down. She worked her hand into his briefs, slowly massaging his muscle. She could feel the blood flow surging to the tip, in the same time fully coming to its full potential. She continued moving her hand from the base to the tip of his muscle. She pulled back just a bit to sneak a peek at what was in her hands. She found an interest in what was in her hands, and in that moment she knew what she had to do." I want you to come for me," she said looking at him dead in the eyes. "I want you to come for me baby," She then increased her stroke and became aggressive. She had a goal make him come, she wanted to take him to that place. ELECUPHORIA, where your body and mind lose control and are unable to connect with any parts of your body. Her grip became more firm, stroke intensified, he could feel the pressure. He didn't want to come, he didn't want to release, if he could just control the situation and just hold back that flow. That flow, his nectar. Mind over matter Dawayne was think to himself," You can't come, not right now!"

He was able to hold back a few more minutes, she put her hands on it. He put his mouth on her nipple, she pulled back, "No, I want you to come." He couldn't hold it any more, he was leaking like a freshly tapped maple tree. Serenity's hand was covered, and he could see the look of accomplishment on her face. She continued her stroke, God it felt so FUCKING good, Dawayne thought. She was able to extract every drop into her hands, and with that she walked to the lavatory. Turning on the faucet and washing her hands, she looked back and he was there right behind her. Pants off and erect as a mother fucker, she didn't even get the chance to turn the water off before his fingers were tracing her folds. He moved his finger inside of her, tapping his finger to the balloon hidden behind the walls, and next to her pubic bone. His movement had purpose, and he knew what he was going for. He was going to make her squirt, he could feel the balloon slowly swell. Once it swells, you are not far from getting her to squirt, he could hear a sound.

Like the sound of water being backed up by a damn, the sound intensified and her balloon became full. It was time, he moved his finger with such speed and such force." I feel like I have to pee," she said, "That's not pee," he whispered. With one flick of the wrist, she squirted, she didn't realize that she did. She noticed she was more wet then normal, this was like trickling down her thigh wet. "What the fuck just happened," Serenity said. Dawayne just looked at her and kissed her, it was so fucking sexy, so fucking hot. Getting her to squirt turned him on, he didn't noticed that getting her off just then caused him to come again. What a turn on he thought, sexy as fuck, she was his lil Bonnie Rotten. Serenity was still unsure of what she had just done, what her body had just gone through. She cleaned up the best she could with paper towels and tried to clean off the look of ecstasy and satisfaction and fix her makeup. He found his pants and cleaned himself up in the men's lavatory, Saying there good byes and kissing good bye. He snuck her out the back again, always going out first to make sure the coast was clear. "All good," he said as she came out the door, he looked at her and saw her beauty. He couldn't resist he had to taste her one more time, he pulled her into him, and kissed her, as he pulled away. He sucked on her lip, and as he pulled her lip, he bit down just a tad. Chills and his electric sexual energy went rushing through her body once more, in her mind she was like take me right now. He fought his own battles with his head. He was wanting to shred the clothes off her and take her right there. Bend her over and go DEEP in Serenity, the thought of it was making her wet and him hard. They knew they didn't have the time to, and couldn't even if they wanted to. They were outside the mess hall, and there could be students anywhere. They kissed one more time and then Serenity went around the corner and vanished from his sight. Soon as she was gone he had this feeling, sad yea, but he felt incomplete. Was she his missing piece, was she the person that would complete him. The drive home, he still had the feeling, something was missing, and that something was her. Meanwhile on campus Serenity had the same feeling, when she was near him she felt safe, felt sure, and felt right about it all.

She hated leaving him, because she knew each time she would have this feeling. Missing him, wanting him, there with her or her at home with him. As these feelings of him bounced around in her head. A Good thing, by Nick Jonas popped up on the radio station. What a coincidence she thought, shit like that happened a lot with him. She could feel his energy from far away, he could sense her vibes from ant distance. Connected on ALL 3 levels of energy, Mental, Emotional, and Physical. What they had was rare, and what they were doing was also so taboo. So risky so dangerous, but they didn't give a fuck, if they didn't get caught, they both thought it must be meant to be. If they get caught so be it then they would have to deal with whatever happens. The next day during dinner Serenity slid him a note, the note read, visit me at work on my lunch break. He was all excited, and just like that a plan came to view.

AFTERNOON
SESSIONS

The day had come, and Dawayne was ready for it. He hoped in the shower that morning with good vibes, he played his music on his phone through his speaker. The music was bumping, and the only thing that was on his mind was her, Serenity. He shaved and washed up, looking through his closet to find the perfect outfit. He went through his closet trying on a pair of pants, then switched to shorts. God how he didn't like wearing pants when it was hot outside but fuck, it went well with the shirt he had on. So he said,"FUCK IT." Put together his outfit and got so fresh and so clean, the affair by Rico Love, burst its way through his cell speaker. "Is this a summer fling or an every summer thing," he sang out loud. Yet intentionally asking himself, if it was a summer fling or an every summer thing. He received the message lunch time at 11:00, he got all excited. The energy that was inside him was urging to explode out, he did his best to take his time getting to her work. He was still really early, nerves he guessed. So he parked so he could see her coming out of the entrance, he sat there sweating. The air conditioning was on, so he had no reason to be sweating. Maybe it was his old friend PARANOIA, it had been a while since she was lurking behind his every move. Dawayne thought that he had gotten rid of her, but yep she was there. He was thinking what if somebody saw him, what if somebody saw them together. Serenity walked out of the entrance, and PARANOIA was bitch slapped to the back to the depth of where it came from. Trying not to show his excitement to much, he fiddled with the car lock and hit lock instead of unlock. He didn't know whether to get out the car and open the door for her, or just let her glide right in. She reached for the door and he hit unlock just in time. He took a deep breath. "Hello Beautiful," he said this was the first time that he and her were together with no familiar eyes to watch out for. They drove about 5 minutes away to a sandwich shop, stood in line and flirted with each other. This was really happening, they were on their first date. They received their order and walked to his car, his drove to the nearest park. So they could enjoy some shade and some perhaps good conversation, or just enjoy her energy. He pulled near some trees and parked the car. Kept the car running for the a/c, turned the music down to a conversation level. They talked and laughed, taking about all the crazy shit they have gotten away with in the mess hall. Holiday was about to come up soon, and the students would leave campus for a few weeks.

That meant that he was going to go a couple weeks without her energy, or him even seeing her. They sipped on their sprite, and ate their sandwiches. That was the day to remember, he waited a day to have lunch with her just building the courage up. This time they got their food and drove to the park, he parked the car and couldn't keep his hands off her. He moved to her thigh, to her waist, from waist to stomach and then chest. Serenity closed her eyes, and exhaled. She pushed his hands back," No we can't," they sat there in his car and then the clouds began to roll in. The thunder began to rumble from across the valley, the lightning pierced its way through the clouds. With the crack and the rumble of the thunder, Dawayne rolled down his tinted windows. You could smell the energy in the air, all the electricity. They looked at each other and the sexual energy between the two of them was thick as promethazine. The water droplet hit the windshield and caught their attention, it began to pour. The rain was cold and demanded attention from whoever was in its path. As the heavenly beads of hydrogen and oxygen slapped, individuals across their faces. Dawayne was engulfed by the blue sexual energy she was giving, his hands started to have a mind of their own. They wanted to feel her, make her wet, make her nipples hard. He got as far as unbuttoning her pants, before they knew it the time was gone. It was time to take her back to work, and he didn't want to leave. This was perfect this was the person he wanted to spend the rest of his life with. Time is a bitch and she was not on their side, he drove her back to work. Serenity dug deep in her bag and pulled out her perfume, she spayed herself and the spayed his entire car. To leave the essence of her lingering in his car, he would have her scent with him until it was no more. The idea popped into his head, to take her to his house. This would be something he would prepare for, taking her to his layer. His mind was in a tornado of crazy sexy, dirty thoughts. The weekend drug way to long, but with her letters they passed back and forth. Dawayne was able to survive, Monday morning he went to the store and bought some supplies. By the time Tuesday came around he was prepared, Serenity messaged him lunch at 11:00. He lit some candles, and put on their playlist, before he went to pick her up. When he got to her work he only had to wait a few minutes, she came out and looked like a Nubian Queen. Straight beauty, her makeup today was on fleek, and her outfit, he wanted to rip it off her. Serenity got in the car, and he started driving to his apartment.

It would be the first time that she would be at his place, they pulled up to his place and it was time to head up. He unlocked the door and followed behind, she went straight to the couch and made herself comfortable. He asked her if she wanted anything to drink, he went to the freezer and pulled out a frosted glass and filled it with water. He then sat down beside her, started up some conversation, the sexual energy between the two was strong. Serenity was in his house, a whole different feeling came over her. Dawayne started messing with her leg, and she flip around on the couch to get away from him. She was behind the couch," Is it alright to flip on your couch," she asked. "Go for it," he said and that's when he attacked. She was flipping over the couch and he got right in front of her, and with his smooth hands he failed the first time to get between her legs. His second attempt he was successful he was where he wanted to be, between them long legs. He unfastened her belt, and began to unbutton her jeans. He grabbed her hips and slid down the length of her legs, while sliding her jeans off of her. She had a black and blue lacy thong on, that was next to go flung to the floor. He put his lips on her legs, kissing and sucking his way down. Starting from the thigh slowly moving to the folds of her sweetness. That chill of arousal and goosebumps took over her body. The sexual energy was so intense, Serenity got up and ran to his room. She looked around and saw the candles, and heard the music. "What is all this?" she asked, he had no answer. He pulled a wrapper out of his pocket, slid it onto his muscle. She fell back onto his bed, and he had his face between her thighs in seconds. He was sucking on her folds, and gliding his tongue in and out of her walls. He started kissing on her hips, tip toeing his tongue up her sides to her breast. He put his tongue on her nipple, moving between both left and right breast. He kissed her neck, and then began to lightly suck, he moved his hips and directed his muscle to her sweet nectar. She gasped as his muscle entered and stretched her walls. His stroke and her stride synched to the music playing in the back ground. As "Coffee," by Miguel played, the two became one in a hot and wet afternoon fuck. The ceiling fan was on high, and was still unable to prevent the sweat beads from forming on both their bodies. Serenity closed her eyes and then opened them, grabbing Dawayne's neck and pulling him in for a passionate kiss. He didn't resist, she began kissing his collarbone. She opened her mouth, placed her lips so softly on his skin and began to suck.

There was pleasure and a slight pain, as she moved along the contours of his collarbone. His thrust and penetration intensified, the slight pain he was feeling turned into pleasure. He was enjoying every moment, and as her teeth pressed up against his flesh. He would grip her plump juicy cheeks in his hands and squeeze, until she applied more pressure. The feeling of teeth in your flesh just a layer away from breaking the skin," God that feels good," he whispered. She was good at what she was doing, finding that point to where he wanted to almost TAPOUT. The mixture of pleasure and pain was euphoric, and having his muscle deep in Serenity was just the cherry on top. Serenity asked what time it was, Dawayne looked 11:50. Shit they only had 10 minutes to get her back to work and it was at least a 20 min commute. She looked for her thong and pants, which were in the living room. She looked at Dawayne and placed her hand on his head, wiping the sweat from his head. This was something that most people would think is sick, but Serenity would just say" It's just sweat!" Then she ran to the living room to get dressed, she found her pants. Her thong was over by the television, she placed her pants on the couch and stepped into her thong. Dawayne got behind her and whispered, "I don't want to take you back to work!" She looked at him and said," Should a could a would a, we can't. She went to the bathroom and fixed herself, "I look a hot mess, like I just had crazy wild sexy," Serenity said. As she was staring into the mirror he was just enjoying the sight that was in front of him. Serenity there in his house, half naked, and sexy as fuck. Her make-up was fucked up but crazy wild afternoon sex will do that to you. Serenity got her items she came with and they were out the door, and down the stair. They got in the car and started the drive back to her job, meanwhile Dawayne was in hog heaven. The whole commute back to her work, Serenity laid her head on his shoulder. Almost falling asleep she grabbed his hand and interlocked fingers. This is how they stayed the whole way back. In the back of Serenity's head she was thinking she could give him road head. It was a great idea, but then could he drive while under her complete control. Today was not the day, to test that idea. Dawayne got her to work, she was only 15 minutes late. They kissed, she sprayed her perfume on her and all over the car. Again leaving her essence to linger in his car, to drive him crazy and only want her more. He watched her get out the car all slow and sexual, she was teasing his black ass.

Until the mirage of her vanish he sat watching, then he put the car in drive and headed back home. Dawayne was high as fuck on love, and lust. He made it to his place and when he opened the door to his apartment, he saw that his living room was destroyed. Walking through his place there was the essence of her all over.

A trail of electric blue sexual energy, intertwined with his blood red sexual energy. Imagine looking at the northern lights bright colors flowing through his house. He laid on his bed, replaying the afternoon in his head. The day had gone almost perfect, only thing missing was her beside him. She was probably on her way back to the campus, and finish the rest of her day without seeing him again. That night he slept like a baby with dreams and vision of his future with Serenity. The morning had arrive and so did the blood to his muscle, his dick was hard as a mother fucker. He began to get ready for another day with his queen, as the hours till he picked her up ticked. In his place, he had the playlist they listened to bumping and vibrating off the walls. The clock on his stove was telling him it was time to leave and pick up Serenity. What was the plan today he thought, he had no idea just live in the moment. Whatever happens, happens he told himself as he pulled up to the front of the building. That day they got lunch, and sat at the park. Serenity was telling him that when she went on holiday where she was going. To her grandparents, she told him that she was going to e-mail him every day. In the back of his mind he was thinking, she'll be too busy with hanging back with friends from home to write him.

He had one more week with her and then she would be gone for spring holiday. Those days went by fast, cause when he went to work on campus he got to see her. Their taboo sexual sessions continued in the mess hall, the secret passing of letters of love did as well. That Monday he woke up early, and decided to bake her something. The first thing that popped into his head was cookie, he went to the grocery store and bought stuff to make chocolate chip cookies. He was so excited and full of life and energy, he had forgot that she didn't like chocolate. He took his receipt and headed to his car, jamming to one of their playlist on the stereo. He got to his apartment and started cleaning up the kitchen, can't cook in a dirty kitchen was his motto. He cleaned what lil mess he had created the night before, and pulled stuff out to make these cookies. In his mind he still forgot that, Serenity didn't like chocolate. Hell his mind was clouded the intentions of doing something to surprise her and make her happy.

He finished making the cookies, and wrapped them neatly for her gift, he also had time to write a lil letter. He went to pick Serenity up from work, and have lunch with her. It was funny they were both thinking of each other, he handed her the cookies and letter. She handed him a letter and a lacy pink camo print thong. He put the thong to his nose inhaled deeply, not realizing what he had just did. "It smells like you taste," he said with a big ass grin. "Thank You, Thank You, he repeated. The gift she just gave him was way better than a fucking cookie, and a chocolate chip fucking cookie at that. She fucking hates chocolate he thought, it was a lil too late to take it back. Plus she gladly took them when he gave them to her and said thank you, letting him know it's that thought that counts. Because once he handed her the cookies, and saw her eyes. He realized what a fuck up he just was, making somebody you love some cookies that she can't even eat. Wow so impressive he thought. "I'll just give them to my sister," she said and "It's the thought that counts." He went the whole morning, and until the time of handing her the cookies. Not thinking that the cookies he made her she wouldn't be able to enjoy. "I'm sorry," he said. That's all that he could muster, that afternoon was an amazing moment. They talked and got lost in the moment, it was that time again. He would have to say his good byes, but this time he wouldn't see her for 10 days. The agony sank to the pit of his stomach, he was going to miss her. Serenity was his missing piece, she completed him. Did he ever tell her that he wondered, he believed he told her? Wrote it in one of his 6 page letters, he thought back to himself. Dawayne looked at the thong that was pressed neatly in his center console. She had left, said her good byes, and completed the ritual she does every time she leaves his car. The fragrance was sweet, it matched the scent of her natural vitamin that extracts from the gland between her legs when aroused. When touched in a very specific way this gland would secrete a nectar, to him it was his vitamin. The very vitamin that he needed to have a daily dose of, he would extract the sweet nectar and could go without a dose for 4 days at most. Going without her nectar for a week and a few days, this was going to be a test. Test his heart, test his trust, a day didn't go by that they didn't e-mail each other. He remembered the first night she was on holiday, she messaged him. His heart began to beat with purpose, beat like a Jamaican steel drum. The rhythm on his heart beat for him. He knew in the back of his mind, that she could not possibly be with him.

For she already had a forever already in her girlfriend, for he was her one and only. He would forever be her one and only, male that she would feel this way about. Yet they both knew that, she was way more into women than men. Dawayne knew what he was getting himself into, he knew Serenity had a girlfriend. He knew about her, and she didn't know that he was extracting her nectar and going deep in Serenity.

SPRING HOLIDAY

Days turned to nights, week to the weekend, they talked almost every day. The Texting back and forth, e-mailing each other. Dawayne thought writing like this was old school, who does this these days. Luckily Dawayne was a romantic and old school, he felt they got to know each other on a whole new level. Days passed and the day he would see her again came near, he would have to go big this time. So many ideas popped into his head, but the best one was going to be a big deal a in the moment kind of gig. The last idea he had he was going to catch her on her way back and surprise her at the Trans station.

WETTTTT UPON
ARRIVAL

The following week Tuesday couldn't came any faster for the two of them. He went to went to a Chinese restaurant and got one of her favorites orange chicken. Dawayne got his go to, Szechwan pork. Went to the nearest fuel station, and got two sprites. Picked her up and took her to one of the many parks they would visit on their afternoon outings. They got to the park, and he popped his trunk. Pulling out a blanket, and closing the trunk. Going to the passenger side door and opening it for Serenity, as she had the food in her hands. They found a spot under the shade, laying there eating their lunch and having some good chit chat. She jumped on his back and he got up on his knees and stood up. Dawayne began spinning in circles, in the action of getting her dizzy. She held on tight, arms wrapped around his neck. She started to let go, and as she was letting go he was trying to prevent her from falling off of him. He slowed his pace, and tried to stop her from falling. Dawayne came crawling to her asking if she was ok, that he didn't mean to drop her. They kissed and went back to their lunch, he started singing a song. A song that he had written about the time they spent together at the park.

> *She be sittin on my lap*
> *Grindin her body slow*
> *Girl we gotta go, back to my place*
> *I'll let you sit it on my face*

The lunch was a success, his hands began to explore her body as she was wearing a thigh length dress. He could smell the charcoal from across the park, some people were out getting the grill started to char some food. They folded up the blanket, and threw away the trash that they created. He opened the door for her and she got in, moving smooth and quick as a humming birds wings. That lunch was special and every moment that they spent together was special. Not to just him but to her as well, another day went by. The mission was for her to come to his place again.

The following Tuesday came and the clock read 20 minutes till eleven. Dawayne got in his car, and set to go get his queen from lunch. He pulled up front and waited only a few, she came out and damn she was looking good. Every time he saw her, his eyes would go straight to them long legs.

He envisioned them wrapped around his waist, and Serenity pinned up against a wall. She got in the car her scent made his mouth water, and blood rush to the tip of his muscle. She gave him a peck hello, and they were off. They started heading in the direction of his place, back at his place he had everything set up. They got to his place, headed up the stairs and he couldn't even wait for her to get into the room. Dawayne attacked, the sexual creature had been caged too long and it was time to feast on his prey. He grabbed her by the waist hoisted her up, she automatically wrapped her legs around him. They kissed and moved around the apartment without a care in the world. Dawayne wanted to rip Serenity's clothes right off of her, and take her right there. He guided her to his bedroom, and sat her down on his bed. He took her flesh into his hands and exchanged his red sexual energy, she took a deep breath and tilted her head back. He took the cuff of her collarbone into his mouth and sucked, licked, and kissed. With very lil effort he unbuttoned her pants, unzipped and slowly pulled them off her legs. Her scent drove him wild, he wanted to taste her nectar, slurp every drip drop from her folds. Her shirt was next, then bra, he took his fingers and traced the imaginary interstate along her body. Taking his time, he made sure not an inch was missed. Starting from her toes he licked, to behind her ear, he traced her body with his tongue. He teased himself by spending too much time near her sweetness, he traced her inner thigh and along the pelvic bone. He adjusted his position, he had become hard and he was laying on himself. He had one condom left and he had to use it wisely. The creature inside him pounced, Serenity didn't have a chance to prepare for what was to happen. He slid the condom on and eased his muscle to the gates of her nectar. He guided his muscle to her outer folds, he slid the tip up and down. She was wanting more, but he loved teasing her. All the times she would tell him, should a, could a, would a. Today there would be none of that shit, he was going to make the most of this moment. She told him to stop being a tease and that's when he went deep and slow. His hips moved to the rhythm of the music in the back ground, and Serenity had her face deep in some pillows. He pulled the pillows from her face and threw them onto the floor, "Let it out, no need to be quite." She tried to pull away from him, she got herself in a bad position. She had her head pinned up against the wall, all while trying to control herself.

They switched from position to position," Oh my God, oh my fucking God," she screamed into the walls. "Right there, right there," Dawayne was putting in work on that pussy, and he was sure if any neighbors where around they could hear. He didn't give a fuck," whose dick is that," he asked Serenity, she couldn't answer the sexual energy too strong and the feeling that was taking over her body. She had lost the ability to speak English, the words, well the sounds that Serenity was making was a good attempt of speaking her first words. Dawayne slowed his pace, and Serenity was able to catch her breath and answer, "Mmmmmm My dick." He came like that, with just those two words he came, he was saturated in sweat. Serenity had already came 3 times so he didn't feel selfish, but he wanted more. He backed out of her and slipped the condom off, tossed it on the floor. He started moving himself around the walls of her sweetness, he slid himself inside. Oh damn he thought to himself, shit feels so much better without a damn condom. He could tell by the way Serenity arched her back that she wanted more, she was laying on her belly and had her ass in the air. He started moving his hips and teasing the pussy again. He would go in, just the tip and then he would pull out, every sixth time he would push his hips down. Serenity took it like a champ, he was in all or nothing. Her back arched, and she started to get away. She was trying to run from coming again, she was half way off the bed. That's when Dawayne hit the spot, she cursed every word in the book, and screamed to the gods. All gods, which ever one would listen, she screamed to them. He felt it, he was going to come, and this was going to be a big load. He asked her if he could come inside her, what he heard was you cannnnnnnnn. He kept his speed up and slapped her ass, her face was in a pillow that she found on the floor. Sweat was dripping from his head to his chin, and then would fall on to the back of Serenity. "Yes, yes, right there, right there, oh god, oh fucking god," she said almost out of breath. He tensed up, "I'm going to come." "Come for me baby," Serenity whispered and with that he lost himself in the moment. Like a volcano he exploded, and that's when reality hit. Serenity asked," Did you just come inside me?" Dawayne didn't know what to say except the truth, he sighed "yes." Serenity said," I said you cannnnnnnnnT." Oh shit came into his head, his sexual creature had taken over and all he had heard was cannnnn, didn't hear the T. He didn't play fair, how you going to ask if you can come inside someone, when you are going ham on that pussy. Meanwhile she can't even speak English, let alone breath. Expecting them to answer a question clearly, he was speechless. Serenity got up and ran to the kitchen, Dawayne was afraid that he went too far. Going in unprotected was not the best thing to do, although it felt out of this world. It was the wrong thing to do, his body was taken over by his inner sexual beast, and he heard cannnnnnnn, the T was there but as an echo. The T was bouncing off the walls of his inner ear, and only stood out when she repeated herself. He took his time and made his way to the kitchen thinking that he was going to be on the shit list. As he went around the corner she was there, taking deep puffs of her inhaler. Her stomach was quaking and her body was shaking, not the reacting he was going for. Serenity told him he was the first guy to come inside her, and that it shocked her. The love making session they just had took so much out of her she needed to take a few hits from her inhaler. Dawayne took a deep breath, paranoia was stopping by to say good afternoon. Who wouldn't be thinking horrible things, it was a mistake. He couldn't take it back, and what was done was done. Serenity looked at him, he looked at her, and they went to the room to get dressed. Serenity encouraged him to put her clothes on for her, Dawayne smiled and did so with pleasure. It was the least he could do, he had just came inside her, and he thought it was going to be way more or a deal than she made it seem. He got her sandals for her, her bag and they headed out the door. The commute to her work was normal, and the energy between the two was still surging. The music played threw the speakers in his car, they held hands and she laid on him always almost falling asleep. The vision of her carrying his child came into view, and with that he felt at ease. If he was to have a child with anybody else he would sure hope it would be Serenity, although life has its ways of working things out in time. It was hot as fuck outside but in the cab of his car it was cool, and he had the girl of his dreams right next to him. He looked at the clock on the stereo, shit time was not on their side. This was the first time he looked at a clock since he brought her to his place. They pulled into the parking lot and said there see you later, and kissed. He watched as she headed to the front to check out, she had a short day today and had forgot. He watched her come back outside and hop on the trolley that would take her back to campus.

HATE GOODBYES

Summer holiday was near, and the emotions the two shared was the same. He didn't want her to go, and she didn't want to leave. The last sexual session they had was not at his apartment, they had many more excursions in the mess hall and on the facility those last few days before Holiday. The day had come and it was time for their good bye's for 3 weeks, 21 motha fuckin days. Serenity had avoided the mess hall all day, but she knew she would not get another chance to see him before she left. The mess hall was empty but there were always those that came late, so he left the doors unlocked. He tried his best to make everything all right, he held her, told her he loved her. He could see the sorrow in her eyes, and she could see that the fire was flickering in his. He held her and squeezed, squeezed so tight, he didn't want to leave. He handed her a card, "Here is a lil something I made for you, along with a version of a scrapbook of the memories they shared. The card had the number counting down from his age to zero, she was to find the number and count her way up when she was overwhelmed. On the other side of the card, some lyrics to their songs on the playlist. She had made him a pile of notes, each note with a specific instruction. One read open when you miss me, another read open when you are stressed. In all there was about 12 letters neatly folded like an envelope. "I will do my best to savor each one and to open one every 3 days. That would be enough to hold hi m off on the natural high he received when her opened and read her letters. He had sent her a message earlier that morning, maybe it was a good plan if he held onto the letters that he wrote her. Just didn't want those letters to get in the wrong hands, or something bad to happen to them while she was gone. They held each other for what seemed like eternity, he felt emotion trying to take over him and he could see the tears running down her face. He loved her and didn't like having to see her so hurt. She had so much going on in her life, she had a girlfriend that she was going to be spending holiday with. When would she have the time to talk to him, message him? She had her and that was that, he remembered the last time they spent together at his place. On the ride home he played her a song, Trade Hearts by Jason Derulo.

He knew that she loved him he was her one and only, and she also loved her. She was her forever, what a battle the heart had he thought. He wished that he could trade hearts, feel the things that he could never feel being him. Feel the things she only felt, he could put herself in her shoes, but to trade hearts that would be sweet. Dawayne believed he would sacrifice himself for her, if he was ever put in that scenario he would do it. No over thinking just react to the way his heart felt, he opened his eyes and she was still there. Tears trickling down her face, he took his finger and wiped the tears away. "I love you," Dawayne whispered as he did that they heard the door click open. The dormitory mother was behind the glass door, and walked into the mess hall. Serenity and Dawayne made a lil distance between each other, "Hey we been calling for you, you're the only one left in the wing." Both their hearts were beating like drums, the adrenaline rush they both had was at peak level. They exchanged I love you's with their eyes and with that she was gone. After locking up the mess hall, he took the long walk to his car. Dawayne wasn't sure if he was hearing and seeing things, or maybe it was his old friend paranoia. He unlocked his car and got in, that was the longest drive home ever. On his way home "I belong to you, and me," by Whitney Houston came on his stereo. He felt his stomach begin to turn, his mouth started to water. He was going to vomit, he took a few deep breaths and slowed his breathing. That's when his eyes began to water, he could not hold his emotions anymore. Dawayne cried and he let it out, his emotions were raw and he was only human. The mixed emotions with not seeing Serenity for 3 weeks, and most of the time she would be spending holiday with her girlfriend. He felt like giving up, why continue the taboo affair. His emotions and feeling that he had for Serenity were too strong to just end to what they had. What did they have? He asked himself, they lived in moment and that's exactly what it was. A moment an indefinite short period of time, he was going to cherish every moment they shared and every moment they made together. Fuck what people would think, or say, they didn't know the story they created. They got to know each other on an emotional, mental, intimate level. With that connection they would forever have that crazy unheard of perfect connection. They were able to read each other's energy, and at times read what the other was thinking. After a long drive home, he walked into his place and hopped into the shower. He turned the nob to red until it wouldn't turn anymore.

The water was hot as lava, but when he stepped into the shower the water seemed to peel his pain for Serenity away. Like an artichoke the heat stripped the layers of flesh from his body, he stood in the shower for longer than an hour. The lights were off and the music played loud through his speaker, he sang out the lyrics to some of the songs as loud as he could. Possibly if he sang loud enough, she could hear the lyrics. The night came and went, the morning came and shined its gloomy face through his window.

SUMMER
HOLIDAY

An extended period of leisure and recreation, especially one spent way from home or in travel. More commonly used overseas, than in the states. The term, in the states uses the word more regularly know is vacation.

Dawayne was doing his morning thing, and cleaning his apartment up and his phone chimed. He always had this strong energy connect with him when Serenity and him were thinking of each other coincide. The chemistry they shared was on a whole other level. He grabbed his phone, caramel praline illuminated across his screen. She had texted him and 24 hours hadn't even gone by. Dawayne got all excited," holy shit," he yelled out with excitement. He unlocked his phone and opened the message it read good morning and I miss you and love you. He replied back oh you don't even now and a good morning to you. That day the messaged each other back almost the whole day, he missed her and she missed him too. The week that she was going to spend with her girlfriend was coming around the corner real fast. Dawayne thought that once she was with her, they wouldn't spend much time chatting with each other. So he prepared himself mentally and emotional for life to bitch slap the shit out of him. The days came when she was with her for the rest of holiday. Dawayne got sick to his stomach, he held on to his stomach. It felt like being stabbed in the guts with a fork, and whoever stabbed you decided to spin your insides like getting spaghetti. Serenity messaged him I made it safe love your face. Those first few hours went by fast, he was lucky he was at work and that keep him busy. All that was on his mind was Serenity, but he was able to finish his shift without any worries. It was when he left work and drove that long drive back home. That energy came over his body again, she was thinking of him and he was of her. A song that was on their playlist popped on the radio, "The affair," by Rico Love. The lyrics so real to the situation or shall I say moment they were creating. Is this as summer fling, or an every summer thing, the lyrics spoke to him and how he was thinking if this moment with

Serenity was a summer fling, or if there was a possibility that it could be an every summer thing? The idea in his head was that if it was a summer fling, it would be just that and he would enjoy each moment as if it was his last. If it eventually became an every summer thing, he would be grateful and appreciate this wonderful moment for the rest of his life. He pulled off the autobahn and hit the roundabout, he had passed his exit and had to go the long way back to his place. His mind wasn't clear and it was clouded with the thoughts of Serenity, and what she was doing. Pulling up to his complex the memory of her and him leaving his place having to take her back to work.

Serenity masked with the scent of his sweat and sexual energy all over, she tried to cover it up with the delicious scent from bath and body works. That scent would always drive him crazy, he would inhale it and the sexual creature in him would be knocking on the door of his conscience. Dawayne paced in his living room, and decided he need to just take a damn shower. He walked to his room, undressed and got ready for his shower, just then he decided to get his notebook out and start a letter to Serenity. He grabbed his fine black sharpie marker and began to write. Before he knew it had had written about 5 pages to her and all while butt ass naked sitting on his bed. He looked at the first page and flipped to the last, then he closed the notebook and turned the hot water on. Went to soundcloud on his phone, and typed the genre r&b and let the lyrics of Eric Bellinger take him away. The room filled with hot steam, and his heart slowed. He felt like his chest was caving in, he took deep breaths and turned the water off. He stepped out of the shower and took his black towel into his hands. Dried himself off walked the four steps to his bed and fell. Dawayne laid there unclothed and let the ceiling fan dry him off, he closed his eyes and breathed deeply. He opened his eyes back up and looked at his phone. 10:24pm illuminated he had feel asleep, almost slept the rest of his night away. The strong energy from Serenity misted him, and his phone chimed that so familiar chime. Sorry haven't emailed you Wi-Fi here is shit, and phone has been charging. Dawayne was just happy that she had even texted him, he thought she would be busy spending some good old lesbian time together. He was just surprised to hear from her so soon he was expecting in maybe a day or two he would see a wyd? He replied back, and they messaged each other until one of them fell asleep. More so of the time she would fall asleep on him and then wake up a few hours later when he fell asleep. The night turned into day, they would message each other while he was at work. She messaged him while watching a movie by herself. Now if she was to be spending the last of her holiday with her, then why would she be spending time watching a movie by herself he thought. If he was there with Serenity there was no way that he would, not spend any moment she wanted to spend with him as the happiest man alive. The summer that was going to hurt like a mother fucker, wasn't as bad as Maroon 5 made it out to be. One day Serenity sent him a picture, not just any picture. He looked at the flesh so smooth, so shiny and freshly inked skin.

With the saying live in the moment across her collarbone. It was the saying that she would always repeat to him when his friend paranoia would take over. To Dawayne tattoos were the sexiest thing a woman could wear, a blank canvas with beautiful colorful artistic stories of people's lives deeply etched into flesh. Dawayne went to the box he had of her letters, the notes that had lil saying on it. He opened the letter that read, "Open when you miss me." He read it took his time, whenever he read any of her letters or notes he would wait till it was time to lay down. To him they were bedtime stories, and they would help him when she wasn't near. He was able to open and read one every four days that helped him ration her sailing love. It took all his might not to open the letters in the first few days, but he was able to manage. The notes and letters kept him alive, the words that he read were like a rush of endorphins. Pleasure, pain, lust, love, were all rushing to his heart, and with an overload of emotions he would fall fast asleep. In his deep sleep he would dream about Serenity and him, dreaming of the possibilities. Each night the dreams would vary, the scenarios would go from erotic to just good vibes. He would wake up refreshed and brand new, waking up and thinking that she would be lying beside him. "Fuck your life," he said. The dreams were so real, he could feel her energy, and her scent wafted across his nostrils. He roll over and she would not be there, so sad his hurt yearned for her. Dawayne would go back and read the letter from the night before, and just reassure himself that it was all real. This thing, this moment that they shared together was real and that's all that mattered to him. Heading to the shower, to get ready for work he would blast the music. Music could always make the situation better, unless Whitney popped up on the radio, or Rico Love. One night Dawayne caught himself going to the Hobby Lobby, he pick up his old hobby and a paint brush. He got her favorite colors, a black canvas to start what he was unsure of. He was going to make her a gift, using his skill in art. He gloated as he left the store, he had an idea. Such a great idea, he was going to incorporate this tree he saw the other day and his love for her in a poem. Dawayne got home, got in some sweats and comfortable t-shirt. He clicked in his I-tunes on Mumford & Sons-Wilder Mind album. He let the music enter his body, he started from the bottom with electric blue. After the album was over, so was he. The tree that he had painted on this canvas had texture to it. Touching the bark of the tree, he made it almost real feeling.

The next night after work he worked on a poem, he was going to paint the letters backwards to that read in a mirror the meaning of the poem would make since. Making sure not to mess up the writing backwards, Dawayne took more time and patience to get every letter perfect. After four days it was complete, he took it to the bathroom looked into the mirror and read. "That's sick as fuck, I can't believe I created this." He was doing the running man, he was so excited and proud of himself. He was hoping that he could force all of his red energy her way, and she would know that he was thinking of her. Even far away from Serenity, they were still able to connect and keep building on to their world of Elecuphoria. A few nights he had caught himself writing her letters, butt ass naked waiting to hop in the shower. Then there were a few nights that he was able to shower and then write his long ass letter. He would continue this letter writing while wrapped in his towel. The day she arrived back on campus, Dawayne had composed a twenty-four page letter. He had the painting and the notebook of his composed letters, he took them with him to work and waited for the perfect time to surprise her with them.

He was excited getting her the notebook would be easy, but how in the hell was he supposed to get the painting to her. It was a good size canvas, yet small enough that it could be placed neatly in a book bag.

That's exactly what he did, during lunch in the mess hall he caught her attention. Dawayne told Serenity that he needed her book bag, he took it to the back and placed the items in the main compartment. Dawayne took a deep breath and headed back to the mess hall. He found where Serenity and Wynter were sitting and he placed the book bag on the floor. "It's all fixed," he said and with that he winked and mouthed I love you. A few moments later he saw Serenity and Wynter leave the mess hall, and hopefully check out what he placed in her book bag. She came back about ten minutes later, and had a big ass grin on her face. "Thank You, "Serenity said. " It's beautiful I love it, and the poem OMG!" Dawayne was glad to see the reaction from her, he knew that he did put in time on his lil art project for her. The notebook of love letters would take a while to read he thought, there were plenty of pages to savor and read. By dinner time Serenity had read all the pages in the notebook, she told him that she couldn't wait. After dinner they didn't have much time to reunite, the good thing was that he was going to see her for lunch in two days.

Dawayne wanted to say, and do so much hell he hadn't seen her for twenty-one days. Fuck he thought to himself, he wished he had done more, showed more emotion. He thought he was going to cry when he saw her, but he didn't. When he was in his car and thought about the moment when he saw her, his stomach began to ache. His mouth started to water, he felt sick to his stomach. He almost vomited in his car, then the tears came. He had held his emotion back to the point of causing himself sick. Dawayne finally made it home, cheeks damp from tears, eyes clouded from emotions. He walked up the stairs to his lonely apartment, forced himself to take a shower and to not think of the should a, could a, would a's of the night. After his shower he laid onto his bed, and did his nightly ritual. Read one of her unread letters, spayed his pillow with her perfume, and closed his eyes to hopefully catch up to her in her dreams. That night he had the craziest dream, they were in the city. The city was bright with lights, they were on a roof top. They were on a roof top of a tall building, the lighting was perfect and the mood was right. She was in a dress electric blue, and he was dressed in all black, with a red tie. Music began to play, and the darkness began to move. Now was his chance, Dawayne took Serenity by the hand and bent down on one knee.

He pulled out a ring and asked her to marry him, the people around waited for her answer everything around him slowed down. Besides his heart beat, it was beating out of his chest. The blood in his veins was flowing bright red, and Serenity's energy was radiating from her body. He knew what her answer was going to be, then he heard a familiar sound in the background. He took her hand and looked into her eyes, and the sound got louder, the sound was getting to close to intense. His ears started ringing, Serenity mouthed her answer. He couldn't hear what she was saying, he started reading her lips, and that's when he woke up. "What a fucked up dream", he said to himself as he forced himself out of bed. The dream was amazing, he wished it to be true, but dreams have a way of flipping your shit upside down. He didn't even get the chance to hear her answer, didn't get the opportunity to put the ring on her finger. He laid their waiting to get in the shower, and he started to write what his dream was about. If anything, Dawayne had to make sure he put this dream down on paper. Whenever he dreamed of her, he realized something. He needed her in his life, no matter if she was his, or hers, he needed her.

He couldn't function without her electric blue energy surrounding his blood red soul. He finished the letter which when done was three pages, folded it and hopped his black ass in the shower. The music bumping through his speakers calmed him down, soothed his emotions. Dawayne headed out the door to his car, and was ready to let life take him by the hand. Throw him into the river, and then grab him by the throat. Force his head under water to drain him from his energy for what was reality. He drove to work that day, with a smile on his face, his heart beating with a purpose, and the feeling of love bubbling in his heart.

BOY SHORTS
& BABY OIL

A few days passed, Dawayne was excited for his next lunch session with Serenity. Summer holiday had tested him, and he aced that mother fucker. He wanted to do something special for Serenity, those little notes from her kept him afloat. He went to the store and bought some baby oil and a candle. In his mind he was going to give her a massage, the best fucking massage she would ever receive. Set the mood right, and just let his fingers glide over every inch of her body. Tuesday had arrived and the mission was to give Serenity the best massage ever, without it turning into a sex session. This would be about her, the beautiful person he had falling in love with and created an amazing moment with. He threw a towel in the dryer, pushed start and headed out the door. That afternoon, Dawayne guided her through his apartment blind folded. Serenity could hear the music get louder as she was guided to the unknown. He whispered in her ear at the doorway to his room," Do you trust me, do you trust me" She said nervously, "Yes." With that he guided her to the side of his bed. He started unclothing her, she was hesitant about this situation. Being blindfolded and be asked of trust was scary and a turn on in her head. She was thinking that some Fifty Shades of Gray shit was about to go down. He pulled her blouse over her head and kept it right where her eyes were. Extra protection her thought, preventing her from seeing all this would only intensify her urges and open the door to her weakness. Dawayne sat her down on the bed, unbuttoning her pants and gently taking them off with his teeth and mouth. He got to her thigh and his lips began to wonder, he started sucking and kissing her thighs. As his red energy started to collide with hers Serenity took in a deep breath and exhaled slowly. Dawayne went back to taking off her pants and as he got to the calves his lips wondered again. Serenity inhaled quickly and held it for what seemed like forever to him. He got to her toes and he could resist, his lips started kissing her toes. Moving his tongue between each toe, Serenity exhaled. The pants were gone, and under was a plump, round, tight, juicy ass.

Black boy shorts, and a bra was all that was left. He was still at her toes, kissing and sucking on them. He looked at the beautiful canvas he was about to work on.

Her body the canvas, his hands and fingers the brush, and the baby oil as the paint. He was about to find his inner Bob Ross and this moment would be remembered for ever in Elecuphoria. He crawled on top of Serenity, taking his time to kiss on sensitive areas of her body. He was straddling her, and his fingers attacked the bra. With two flicks the bra was off, and he slowly took that off her shoulders. Lifting her up slightly too only throw the bra across the room, he whispered." I'm not going to fuck you, I'm going to explore your body!" Dawayne placed his hands under Serenity's boy shorts and squeezed. Moving his thumbs between the cracks of that ass, he spread her legs open. Just enough to get his hands on her inner thighs, he then moved to her waist. Grabbing the elastic band with his teeth, moving from side to side, and pulling till the boy shorts were completely off. He threw them with his left hand, and with his right he pulled out the baby oil he had hidden by his bed. He then slid beside Serenity, and with one quick motion he was in control. He popped the lid, squirted a large amount in the palm of his hand. Rubbing his hands together activating the ingredients that caused the oil to heat up. He moved his hands to the concave in her neck, and his fingers began to dance in sync along the vein in her neck. He applied pressure and slowly crossed his fingers into each other. Dawayne's fingers glided to collarbone and his fingers pranced on the length of her shoulder. Making sure to brush over every visual baby fuzz, brushing his fingers back to the base of her neck. Serenity exhaled, the sound of a lower vertebrae popping back into placed echoed. As Serenity arched her back in pleasure, she hiked her sweet ass right in his face. His lips attempted to kiss those sweet cheeks, but his lips were two inches to far to indulge on that sweet ass. His hands went straight on attack mode, his fingers squeezed into the flesh of Serenity. She bit her lip in excitement and her sexual energy radiated her canvas. He went back to work on her body, adding more oil and more pressure to outer edges of her vertebrae. His fingers slid along the length of her spine, and his fingers tip toed slowly up to the base of her neck. Dawayne did the motion numerous time, and every time his fingers got to the base of her ass he stopped breathing.

Serenity's ass was a weakness to him, his fingers could wonder off at any moment when that ass was naked. Her legs his kryptonite, those wrapped around his shoulders or his waist got him every time. He was able to keep from wondering and continue the mission. He took his time going from shoulders, to arms, to back, and when he was done working on the upper body he moved below the waist. He focused heavily on the juicy ass in his hands, with wet warm fingers he slid his fingers along the walls of her sweetness. Slowly moving from her bottom cheek to the top of her ass. He slid back down to the outer walls, he could feel her warmth. His fingers skimmed along the warm wet walls, he slowed his pace when he got to her thighs. His fingers moving the same pattern on each thigh, his fingers opened wide. Covering more surface was key, sliding up and down the length of her leg. He brushed the baby hairs on her calves, flicking his wrist to move the curves of her ankles. He took her right foot in his hand, adding oil to her foot. He moved his hands and fingers into the wrinkles in her foot. Each finger had a place between her toes, and moving about. He grabbed for the candle that was at the head of his bed, he then tipped the candle. As he tipped the candle the red hot wax pierced her skin. She arched her back in surprise, he poured more between her shoulders. He massaged the wax onto her skin, the wax broke into small flakes. As the flakes moved around and settle in place. He had placed a towel in the dryer before he left for this exact moment. He came back to the room and with a fresh warm towel he cleaned the hardened wax off her body. Going back to her feet he made sure her feet where well hydrated he flipped her onto her back. That was nigga shit, he would pull every now and then. When she lease expected it, his sexual creature would take over. It look every ounce in his body not to slide upside that sweetness. He maintained the amount of lust awakening inside of him. Her nipples hard and erect, her stomach slowly rising and falling. Such a beautiful sight, he stopped to take a moment and just admire what was lying there. He searched for the bottle of baby oil, found it on the floor. He then closed the lid, shook, opened and squirted it on her back. Saturating her back in oil, his fingers began to work their magic.

Moving along the noticeable veins under her skin, they moved telling a story. Only a second passed in reality, some way in this moment time was able to slow down. Magic or phenomenon whatever you may call it, it happened this afternoon. Serenity could feel the blood flowing to his muscle, it was pulsating. How long he was going to be able to control sexual creature and just fuck me, Serenity thought. His hands moved around her body, making sure to brush every inch with his sexual ora. Leaving a trail of sexual red energy illuminating his canvas. He reached for the candle again, dripping hot red wax on her stomach, and between her breasts. He placed a dab of baby oil in his hands and worked his way to the hardened wax. Pressing his fingers deep into her flesh the wax broke into sections, and once it was all broken up he retrieved the still warm towel and cleaned her up. He looked at the time on his phone, and searched for her boy shorts. He took putting them back on her in his hands, she was still blind folded surprisingly. He then found her bra, placed the straps over her shoulders and clipped in place, He then got her pants, placing both feet in first and moving up the length of her legs, to her ass. Her bubble prevented him of putting them on with ease, she lifted her hips and they wear around her waist. He zipped up and buttoned the single button. Looking for her blouse, Serenity took off the blind fold. "I was scared, I thought you were about to do some Fifty Shades of Grey shit," she said. "I wanted this moment to be all about you, no sex, just enjoying your body," Dawayne said quietly. She said" Thank You," and they were off to take her back to work. She fell asleep on him on the commute, they said their see you later. Never good byes, good byes are if you think you will never see that person again. There were only two days a week he didn't see Serenity, and yea those days were hard. Yet those were the days he would read the letters they wrote to each other. Dawayne was comfortable with were his life was heading and the word comfortable was something he steered far away from. In past relationships he never wanted to be comfortable, because once you're comfortable with your situation you have tapped out. A moment or relationships should always grow, never be easy. Complicated sometimes, but hell he was sharing a moment with Serenity even though Serenity had her girlfriend. The word complicated was probably the best way to define what the two of them were. He watched her go throw her bag, find her perfume and do her ritual.

Every time she got out of his car she would do this, leaving his with a lust and hunger for her even more. He pulled away with a smile on his face, he had completed the mission. He was able to give Serenity a full erotic, sensual body massage without giving in to the sexual animalistic creature that lurked in the shadows of his mind. He was able to control the savage sexual beast with in him, and not give in. He had a great day after their session, no sex and still satisfied. He went to bed that night with a heart full of lust and lungs full of her scent. Time flew by quick, next thing he was at the mall with Serenity, they were walking by the Victoria Secrets outlet. Serenity grabbed his hand, and guided him through the store. She grabbed a bra and panties, pulling him to a dressing room. She turned and took off her shirt, and then her bra. Pulling down her leggings she had no thong on, Dawayne pulled her in by the hips. Sliding his muscle into her damp walls, he began to thrust. In the middle of his thrust, there was a knock on the door. Serenity yelped out a chopped, "yes." The Victoria Secret associate began knocking harder on the door, and then they heard a sound that stopped both of their hearts. Keys began to jingle, and the door knob started to rattle. The door opened up and there stood Autumn, a green eyed goddess. Jet black hair, in her associate attire and breast pleading for the top button to pop off. She closed the door behind her, and said" It looks like you two could use a lil assistance." Dawayne with his pants down and Serenity fully undressed both stared at each other. Autumn took Serenity by the neck, and began kissing her collarbone. Dawayne started to feel the blood rush back to the head of his muscle, and became very aroused by what his eyes were seeing. Autumn asked Dawayne if he liked what he saw, bobbing his head up and down like a fool he agreed. Autumn then took her lips and started licking on Serenity's neck, and moving down to her chest. There she focused on serenity's hard brown nipples, and asked again. "Do you like what you see?" What the fuck was happening, Dawayne thought was this a dream. If this was a dream he would for sure die a happy man if it ended the way he thought it would. He whispered, "Yes." With that Autumn pulled her work attire off, and underneath a Jamaican ocean blue bra peered through. She then pulled off her tight black dress slacks, and to his surprise bright red thong with coral blue illuminated the dressing room. At this time Serenity was still in shock, but was enjoying every second of this freaky coincidental out of this world sexual experience.

In a fucking V.S fucking dressing room, Autumn then pulled her thong down and stepped out of them. Autumn put her arms behind her and pulled Dawayne into her, she was wet as fuck. So fucking wet so fucking wet, she then grabbed Serenity by the head and slammed her face into her juicy breast. Serenity's automatic response was to start sucking and kissing her breast. Dawayne slid in and out of the newly discovered caverns of Autumn, his muscle pulsated with each stroke. His muscle had been hard before, but he had never felt it this hard before. He felt as if his muscle had grown to thirteen inches. Her caverns were so wet, so unexplored, he continued his stroke. Serenity was gasping for air, Autumn's breast were at least a DOUBLE D. Serenity saw the look in Dawayne's eyes and then she began to bite on Autumns nipples, trying to get the attention on her. It worked Autumn moved away from Dawayne, and put one leg up on the lil seat and twisted. Forcing Serenity's head to her cavern, Serenity gasped and looked at the art that was on her leg. Autumn had a mural tattoo of Fat Albert and the Cosby Kids on her leg. A shimmering clit piercing that was calling to be played with. Serenity dove in, unable to hold back the urge of tasting unknown territory. Autumn tasted like RED Kool-Aid, on a hot fucking day. Serenity explored this uncharted cavern with her tongue, and moved her hands to grip onto a bubble butt. While Serenity was indulging on Autumns natural juice, Autumn then took Dawayne into her mouth and began to stroke. Dawayne could feel her tonsils and beyond, damn she could deep throat some dick. He pulled her in closer to enjoy every inch, he wanted to make her gag. Not tonight, Autumn had no gag reflex and he could see himself in her neck. As the intensity of the dome continued, Autumn started grinding her hips. She was grinding her hips with such speed that Serenity's tongue couldn't keep up. Autumn's hips moved with such speed, that Dawayne caught the speed and began pulling her head into him with the same speed. The creature inside erupted from within, he then took Autumn and forced her on to her knees, and pulled Serenity in front of him. He looked into Autumns piercing green eyes, and said," I want you to taste her, tell me what it taste like." Autumn then put her face into Serenity's sweetness, and with that Dawayne pulled himself into the sweetness that was familiar yet new and freshly polished by a V.S green eyed vixen.

Dawayne felt a pressure pushing him out, he attempted to continue his action.

The pressure was to strong, he pulled out and Serenity squirted like she had built a dam and the wall finally broke. Dawayne forced Autumn to be sprayed by Serenity's nectar, it was so warm, so much nectar. Autumn put her fingers inside herself, and began to flick her wrist, in what seemed like 3 seconds Autumn started to squirt. She pushed on her clit and aimed for Serenity, her stomach was pelted with Autumn Kool-Aid. Dawayne got misted with a lil bit, a drip landed on his bottom lip. He sucked in his lip and tasted an unfamiliar sweetness, unable put his tongue on it he savored. In that second he had a flashback.

THE ORIGINS OF A SEXUAL SAVAGE

Before we get too far ahead of ourselves, we need to ask how did Dawayne become such a savage at his sex game. How did he get to become so familiar and knowledgeable with the female anatomy?

Let's go back to Dawayne's senior year in High school, he was working at nearby grocery store as a bagger. School was almost out and it was almost time to leave home and start a new chapter in college. The bad thing is that Dawayne was unexperienced, he didn't have many girlfriends in school. He was more vested in work and making money, and sports. He had took a girls virginity in the back of his Bronco II, with his fingers. His dick had never got wet, well there was the time that Monica had gave him head in the park in his Bronco. It was sloppy and she swallowed all of him like a champ, but she had been chasing him ever since he switched schools. The first day he arrived, she had put a note in his locker that said...

Welcome
Glad to have some dark meat here
I want to fuck the shit out of you
Just being honest and you sexy as hell
You don't have to find me
I'll find you

That was Monica, she was into black guys, and Dawayne helped her full fill her fantasy or whatever was on her check list. Let's get back on track though, during the summer there was a young woman that would come in to the grocery store. She would always make sure she went to the register that he was bagging at, and have him escort her to her car with a small cart of groceries. Well one hot day, she introduced herself to him. "I know you bag my groceries every day, and I know your name is Dawayne."" Only because your name tag, my name is Savanna." "Pleasure to finally introduce myself to you, I have a question would you be interested in having dinner or a drink with me tonight?"" You don't have to answer right now, just meet me at J's tonight at 8:00pm if your answer is yes. "Baffled by what Savannah had said, he looked and didn't want to be rude.

He replied back,"ok." He put the two grocery bags in her trunk and she slipped him a five dollar bill in his apron, like she always did.

Dawayne smiled and said his thank you, and rolled the cart away collecting any straggling carts in the parking lot. He thought about what she had asked him the rest of his shift. He got off of work that night at 5:00pm, he had the early shift that Monday. Dawayne drove home, hell he still lived with his parents. He was eighteen years old, and was a virgin. Virginity was the last thing that he worried about, he would lose that in his own time. Tonight was not going to be that night, Savanna was an older woman at least twice his age. Savanna was very attractive, and had beautiful piercing green eyes, long black hair and body art covered a large portion of her body. He had three hours to decide if he was going to go to J's, he took a shower with the intentions of just getting into some comfortable clothes and chillin with his crew. He hopped out of the shower and dried himself, applying deodorant and brushing his teeth. Dawayne walked to his bedroom and started looking for the right outfit to go to J's. He pulled off the shelf a pair of jeans, and a white T off the hanger. He put on a pair of basketball shorts, and a T-shirt. There was no way he was going to put on what he picked out, with two and a half hours till he had to make a decision. Dawayne put on a movie, but it seemed that time was going by slow. He just wanted 8 o clock, to be hear already so he knew what the fuck he was doing. He left the house and decided to just drive around, if anything that would for sure make time go by. He drove around, felt his stomach hurt. He looked at the time on his stereo, 7:15 illuminated in red. "Shit time went by fast," Dawayne said in a whisper to himself. He drove home and put on the clothes that he had picked out, brushed his teeth again, and sprayed a lil cologne. On his way out his mother told him the usual, be home before the sun comes up. His mother had no problem with him being home late or early in the morning, his G.P.A was high. He already had been accepted to college full ride scholarship and had a job lined up for when he started, so his mother had no worries about her son. Dawayne, took his time driving to J's he made it there with plenty time to spare. Fifteen minutes early, and to his surprise Savanna was already there. She saw him and waved him her way, he got to the booth and sat down across from her." Would you like something to drink," Savanna asked. "French Vanilla cappuccino," Dawayne replied and Savanna started the conversation after.

Her first question was how old are you," eighteen Dawayne replied. Dawayne could see something working in that head of Savanna's once she got her answer. He told her that he was heading to college in August, and was working to save money for that. The waiter came to the table with his cappuccino, told him it was hot and asked if they needed anything else. Savanna asked Dawayne if he wanted anything to eat, told him he should eat to build up his energy. He was good, the cappuccino was all he needed and he wasn't that hungry. Savanna encouraged him to get anything, something. Dawayne ordered a burger and fries, Savanna ordered a bowl of fruit. They continued their conversation were they had left off, Savanna asked Dawayne. "How old do you think I am?" He replied back," Maybe twenty-four, twenty-five." She laughed a lil bit, and she said," Damn honey I wish, but I am thirty-four." Savanna then told him about her life, that she moved here from Florida. Savanna told him that she had a three year old daughter, and that she lived alone. Her daughter was with her parents for a few days, and that she lived about 30 minutes away. She asked him if any of that scared him or made him uncomfortable, he was honest and told her that he didn't mind. Their food arrived at the table and they began to eat their food, in between bites of fruit and food that held a conversation. "You're really mature for your age," Savanna told him. Dawayne told her that she could thank his mother for that. His mother had always had high expectations with him, and he was able to reach them 95% of the time. Dawayne's mother was a strong independent black woman, and raised her son to be a gentleman, and respectful. Savanna told him that it sounded like he had a good mother, he then told Savanna the story of when they moved to Rawlins. His mother the first day they moved there told him he had two options to get a job, or head across the bank to the prison.

Dawayne had been in a lil trouble in the past, so his mother had to set guidelines and boundaries. He continued his story, the first day of school, right after school he had to work. The night they pulled into town his mother told him to get an application from a few places, she told him to fill out the application there that it showed persistence. He got a call the next morning asking him to come in for an interview, he nailed it and had a good start of a resume because before he moved he had two jobs. They had giving him good references, and he knew that he was a hard worker. His first day, after school was out he drove to the restaurant and clocked in.

Savanna was really impressed by his work ethic and dedication towards life. Savanna then looked at him and asked," Do you have a girlfriend?" "No," replied Dawayne, I'm a busy guy, I'm in athletics, have a job, making that money trying to just focus and reap the rewards that may follow." Savanna nodded and said," Damn, a guy with his priorities straight and you're only eighteen?" She looked at him with intensity, he could feel her energy. It was strong and an electric emerald green. Dawayne looked at her and asked, "What?" "Why you looking at me like that," Savanna told him that she was intrigued was all. "Intrigued why?" Dawayne asked Savanna was unsure if she wanted to tell him. Savanna was looking at Dawayne with the Fuck Me Eyes, she then looked at him and said," I want to RAPE you!" "Bring it on," were the words that came out of his mouth. He knew what he had said but didn't really think of it at the time. Savanna then said," You don't you get it, I want to FUCK the life out of you!" "Yea, I heard what you said, and I said bring that SHIT on!" She then put money on the table and said," Follow me home then." She got in her Land Rover, and he got in his Bronco and followed her on the autobahn, the drive was about thirty minutes. They pulled into a small town, traveled a few block up a hill and to the left she turned into a driveway. He pulled in behind her, looked at the time on his watch it read 9:00pm. Savanna got out of her Rover and waited for him. She then got her house key and opened the door, she gave him a lil tour of her house. She made sure to offer him anything to drink, and went to the stereo to put on an album. Berry White bumped through the speakers, Savanna lured him into her bedroom. She then told Dawayne to make himself comfortable, he sat at the edge of the bed and tried to be cool, act cool. She then got down on her knew and asked," Do you mind?" As she went for his belt, he said no. She then told him that she was going to show him what to expect when a woman pleases a man. Savanna pulled his pants off, and saw he had no underwear on and saw that his muscle was erect. "Damn, no prep needed," she then put her succulent lips on his muscle. She applied pressure and asked if he like it. "That feels fucking amazing," Dawayne said quietly. She then pulled her mouth off of him and spit into her hands and spit on his muscle, Savanna stroked his muscle for a while and then she went back to sucking him. Like she was trying to get the last drop of juice out of a juice box, squeezing and sucking at the same time. She then asked him if he was going to come, his answer "I don't think so."

She then looked at him and attempted to take his shirt off she was having complications so she ripped it off him. Luckily it was just his undershirt, he had already taken his white T off when she told him to get comfortable. As the next song, "Sexual healing," by Marvin Gaye came on she pounced on him. She then said, I'm going to teach you how to please a woman, and the she straddled his face. Dawayne had never tasted pussy in his life, and when his tongue slid inside Savanna moaned. The taste, the taste was unexpected it was sweet and creamy, like a dessert. He couldn't put his finger on the taste, but if all pussy tasted like this he could eat it for hours. Dawayne eyes wondered for a clock, he was wondering how much time had passed. An alarm clock at the head of the bed read 11:00pm. Two amazing hours had passed by and he had plenty of time to enjoy this experience before he had to be home. Savanna guided him with her hips, and told him things to do with his tongue that a woman or a girl his age would enjoy. She then told him," Always ask a woman if you're hitting their spot, or if it feels good." You don't want to be that guy that can't please a woman, and you assume she is enjoying it because she moans." Moans can be faked, but if you can make their body go into convulsions, their legs shake, make them do things to get away from you. You have to ask one question and one question, to know if you're giving them pleasure or pain.

"Do you like that?" If you ask that question and they say yes, keep going, if they say it's too much ease up on her and let her set the pace. If so you are doing the right thing." Those things are harder to be faked, and when you give a woman that kind of orgasm they will remember you as the one that communicated and knocked that pussy out." Dawayne was taking mental notes as she surfed her pussy on his tongue as he created waves. While riding his tongue she had already lost control of her body twice, screamed out to the heavens numerous times. Bodies saturated in sweat, and the sexual energy in the room illuminated with emerald green and red. Savanna began speaking a language that he could not understand, it sounded like Spanish with a lil twist. Dawayne had her speaking in tongue, he was able to transport her to another world, to another time. "Fuck," she screamed, "What the fuck are you, and where the fuck did you come from?" She told him that he had made her come more times than anyone has ever, and asked if this was his first time." First time," Dawayne replied. "No fucking way," Savanna questioned," For real I have no reason to lie."

"Well either you have beginners luck, or you're a natural born pussy eater," Savanna said. Savanna then turned her hips around and faced the foot of the bed, she slowly slid her pussy lips down his face. She pulled up and then dropped it on him, he stuck his tongue out. Using his tongue like a hockey stick, and the pussy being a puck he slapped it around and went for the GOAL." Oh my fucking God, son of a fucking bitch." Savanna bent over and placed Dawayne's muscle in her hand. She spit on it, and started pumping it like she was trying to extract oil. While she was trying to get him to bust a nut, he grabbed her by the hips and pulled her pussy into his mouth. He flicked his tongue, swirled his tongue, he ate that pussy. He ate that pussy until he felt her legs shake, she began to start sucking harder and harder. Long deep strokes, tons of spit, tons of pressure. Dawayne used all his might and held Savanna down, her legs shook, and she screamed out, "Holy fucking shit, Holy fucking shit." In the back ground you could barely hear Marvin Gaye singing let's get it on. He felt her body tense up and then a trickle of sweet cream entered his mouth. He had made her cream, and cream hard it slowly escaped her body like a maple tree being tapped for its sweet syrup. He caught himself slurping up the cream, it was sweet and tasted so fucking good. "Oh no you didn't, and then she attacked his dick with her mouth. She became aggressive, the slight pain and the euphoric feeling of pleasure he came. She got to the tip of his muscle and using her teeth she scraped the remaining come off, and using her tongue she circled the circumference of his muscle and took him ALL in her mouth. Gagging, and eyes watering Savanna swallowed his troops. Dawayne's toes curled, his ass clinched, his hips moved off the bed. Savanna took him in her mouth again, eyes watering and all, and gagging, she cleaned him up real good. Real fucking good, Dawayne's eyes caught the time on the alarm clock. It illuminated 2:12am, "Holy hell," Savanna screamed. She rolled off of him and slowly crawled to the head of the bed, legs still quivering and arms barely able to hold her up. Savanna made it to the head of the bed, "Damn, Damn, Damn," she said where the fuck are you from, like what planet did you come from?" Dawayne chuckled, "I'm from Casper." She laid there for a few and pranced her fingers over his chest, "Distant Lover," by Marvin Gaye was playing loudly in the back. Dawayne was surprised because during it was the first time he realized how loud the music really was.

He thought back to the moments that had just happened, and when he could barely hear the music playing over the screams, moans, and unfamiliar language Savanna conjured from within. Savanna looked at him and asked, "Ready for round two?" She looked down at his muscle it was still erect," Well God damn, you aren't sore or anything honey," she asked. "Fuck no," Dawayne replied. "Well then," she said laying there on the bed and said, "I want you to FUCK the life out of me!" She then asked him if he had any condoms," If you don't I just bought a box today, for just in case there in the drawer under the alarm clock." He went to the drawer glanced at the clock again, 2:20 am. He opened the drawer and pulled the box out, opening the package you would've never know he was a virgin. Dawayne was trying to keep his cool, and not let Savanna know that he didn't really know what he was doing. Amazingly he opened the box, pulled out a golden wrapper and put on the condom with no problem. "Love TKO," by Teddy Pendergrass echoed off the walls of the room. He then slowly climbed on top, and she grabbed his muscle and rammed it inside her. Dawayne began moving his hips to the rhythm of the music playing in the back ground. Hell he didn't know what the fuck he was doing, but the rhythm of the song kept Savanna satisfied. She moaned, and whispered," Give it to me baby." Dawayne pulled almost out and started long slow strokes, the tip of his muscle would almost escape her lips as he moved away from her. As he came close to her, Savanna exhaled slowly, like what she was getting was too much. Then as he felt the base of his muscle he slammed down on her pussy. She screamed out," Oh my fucking God. "He continued with this action, she was enjoying it and shit he was doing the damn thing for his first time. Then the song changed, Dawayne almost lost his stroke. A familiar song came on," Saving all my love for you," Ms. Houston. He was back in the game, his hips moved to the beat. Savanna's moans grew louder and louder, again she started screaming to the Gods. Dawayne thought to himself that it wasn't as scary as he had made it out to be. Sex, fucking, love making, whatever this was that he was doing was the best feeling in the world. To give and receive a pleasure such as this why did he wait so fucking long? This moment had to happen, he had many chances, but with a mature woman, a mother fucking woman almost twice his age. He was learning things about himself and the female anatomy, that he was sure would help him and guide him for the rest of his adult life.

Every song that was on the album that morning he was able to keep his sexual rhythm with. Savanna then rolled on top of him and took charge, pussy still engulfed by his muscle she had a different rhythm all of her own. His hips glided from side to side, and she slid up and down on him. Dawayne rose his hips, lifting Savanna off of the bed, and submerging ALL of himself deep inside. She screamed out," Holy fuck, God damn, son of a bitch." Dawayne, then asked," How does that feel?" "Fucking, fucking, fucking, fuckingggggggg, Oh my fucking God, it feels AMAZING!" He continued his movements, and she followed his lead. He slowly brought her back to earth, and she had to get off. She asked him if he wanted a drink of water, "I'm good," he replied. "Holy shit look at the time it's 4:30, do you have to be home soon? "I don't have to be home until the sun rises," he told her. "Well God damn, I better hurry up and get a drink so we can continue." Savanna then walked to the kitchen, Dawayne was looking at her ass, so fat, so juicy like a Palisade peach. Just makes your mouth water, and makes you want more, she peered through the doorway, asking again if he was thirsty." Oh I'm thirsty but I don't want to get a drink of water," he said. She then came into the room, and said" I'm going to ride that cock, till you tap out." She pulled him down to the edge of the bed, turned around and grabbed his muscle and slowly guided it to her sweet cream. Savanna rode him reverse until the clock read 6:15, Dawayne had about thirty minutes to get home before the sun came up. "Let me give you my number," Savanna said. As she put her name into his cell phone, he looked around the room to find his clothes. "That was, that was some hell of a time," Savanna said. She grabbed him before he went out the door, and kissed him and told him that she would see him soon, real fucking soon. That summer Dawayne became a man, he visited Savanna between three to five times a week. A large percentage teaching going on, a shit ton of on hand learning, one on one learning. He put some miles on that Bronco, many many many booty calls. Dawayne didn't even care he was being used by this older woman, he took all of what she taught him.

CAUGHT UP

Buzz, buzz, Dawayne's phone at 6:00am. He looks at it text message reads...

I hope you're awake
Somehow someone said something
They want me to talk to the Dean
They're going to talk to you
Just know I got you
I love you
Hope you still have a good morning

Dawayne looked at his phone, he read the texts read them again, and again. In his mind he was freaking out, he had to find a way to calm the fuck down. He went to the letters she had written him, looked at everything that she had given him. He was able to calm himself down, he rolled out of bed and went straight to the bathroom. Turned on the shower, put it on the hottest setting and hooked up his phone to the speaker. Letting the music take him away he hopped in the shower. Washing all the tension, and paranoia away. Dawayne came out the shower, no longer paranoid fool. Funky fresh and with a," It is what it is," attitude on his shoulders. If it's meant to happen it will happen, and that was for both the good and the bad. All Dawayne knew is that he loved Serenity and he knew he would do anything for her, and she would do the same. Serenity became his ride or die, he found his bad bitch and she was one-hundred. He walked to his closet and put on his uniform, heading to the kitchen he grabbed a yogurt and keys and headed off to work. The idea of being caught was far back hidden in his mind, he was going to tell the truth and that was it. If he got in trouble he got in trouble, when he got to work he saw a police car. That made paranoia slap him in the face, his heart almost escaped from his chest. He pulled out his wallet, and looked at the card she had made for him. He counted and repeated positives words, he then walked to the mess hall and clocked in. It wasn't long into Dawayne's shift that he got called up to the Deans office. He knocked on the door and waited for the reply," Come on in," he heard from the other side. Right there he told himself, if this shit goes down he could give to shits. As long as he had Serenity in his life, and she was his he could die a happy man. He walked into the office and beside the Dean was the vice president and three other people in the room. He looked side to side, looking for the officer. No officer in site, Dawayne exhaled slowly and quietly.

"Mr. Jefferson," "could you take a seat."
"We have some rumors that are going around
about you and one of the students."
"Ms. Serenity Williams"

That morning, Dawayne answered every question they had for him with nothing but truth. He thought about swinging the truth, but all the questioned they had him answer. Weren't even the questions he thought they were going to ask him? So he was surprised, that the questions weren't more in depth, or that it would take longer than fifteen minutes of his time. This day changed Serenity and Dawayne for every, it tested their love and honor to each other. The days, after were hard on both of them, they couldn't express how they felt to each other like they had before. Dawayne had come up with a code, one finger meant I love you, two fingers mean I'm thinking of you, a fist meant I want to hold you right now but I know we cant. The days turned into weeks, and the weeks into months. They tried their best to stay on the down low, Dawayne couldn't take it anymore. Why come he couldn't be seen talking to her, or just saying hell? This was bull shit, and the only reason they were on his shit was because he was fairly attractive, and being a young black man. Sure was strange that other faculty could talk to students in the same way and they wouldn't get pulled into the Deans office. In the back of his mind he said," This is some bullshit, how you going to profile me like that."

One night he passed Serenity a note,

I need to see you,
Touch you, hear your voice
This shit is killing me

That night they had good conversation, there was still people in the mess hall and they weren't doing anything bad. Serenity was there with her friend Wynter, who was the only person that knew what they were doing. The mess hall emptied and Wynter left her friend. They talked about how much not being able to communicate with each other was killing them. Serenity told him that she was getting her shit together and going to be done in less than two months. He was so excited, so happy, what was the next step. Serenity was going to find a place to work first, then find a place to live. Dawayne asked her," Are you doing this for me, because of me, or is this what YOU want?" "This is what I want," Serenity said with confidence. Dawayne said, "As long as this is something you want, and you're not thinking this is what I want we are good." Then the door opened, Dawayne's heart fell out of his chest. It was Professor Porter, he taught sports medicine on campus.

He asked Dawayne if anyone was in the mess hall with him, Dawayne replied back. "Yes, yes there is, Serenity is in here with me, we're just talking." Come up to my room when you get done here." He looked at Dawayne looked at Serenity and then left the mess hall. Dawayne looked at Serenity, and then said," Well I better get a good night kiss for good luck." Serenity looked at Dawayne, told him she loved him and kissed him. Her electric blue energy surrounded him, he get a lil twitch in his pants. Knowing that he couldn't, they couldn't not right now, he held her tight and said his see you later. He watched her leave the mess hall, thinking that it may be the last time he would see her. He realized he was doing nothing wrong, like talking to a student was only that. Talking to a student, he knew the rules and he had not broken any of them. He knew what the Dean had told him when they talked to him, he wasn't putting himself in a situation that he couldn't get himself out of. Dawayne locked up the mess hall, turned off the lights and headed to the other side of campus to talk to Professor Porter. Dawayne walked down the hall way, till he saw the sign that read" Professor Porter." He knocked on the door, and he could hear the professor from behind the door saying to come in. Professor Porter was moving some things around and asked Dawayne to take a seat. Dawayne sat down in the big leather chair, the professor asked if he would like some tea. Dawayne replied back, "No thank you." Professor Porter asked him what he was doing in the mess hall with a student alone. "Just talking that was all, talking about music and the music scene outside of campus. The Professor told him some stories of how he use to get pulled in by female students, telling him they would do this for extra credit, and do that to raise their grade. "You can't fall into their traps, they will open up to you. Then they have a hold on you, they have something on you until they graduate." Dawayne told the professor that it wasn't anything like that, that he made sure that he wasn't getting to close to students." I'm just here to do my job, and do it to the best of my capabilities."" I don't need any distractions to get me derailed from my work in the mess hall." The professor talked Dawayne for an hour and a half, telling stories, and telling him if he was going to do things. Make sure that he did them on the down low, do them on the outside of campus. Just to cover his own ass," I don't care what you do outside of this campus, but on this campus keep it professional!" Those were the last words the professor said, and with that Dawayne saw himself out of the office.

As he walked down the hall, he chuckled. Thinking to himself that was the craziest conversation he had ever had with any of the faculty since he has worked there. Soon as Dawayne stepped outside he took a deep breath, held it for as long as he could then he exhaled. Breathing in that fresh air in through the nose, opened his mind to what had just happened. He had almost got caught up, luckily he wasn't doing anything that would've got him more than a talk. He knew when he gave Serenity the letter that he was going to leave the mess hall unlocked. Just in case somebody decided to sneak up on the two of them in the act of some wild and taboo freaky sex session. He just had that feeling earlier that day that something like this would happen, and it fucking did.

Luckily Dawayne went with the vibes and energy he was feeling, it had been a long time since he did touch her, kiss her taste her. He began thinking on his walk to his car, when was the last time he got to taste her sweet nectar. Wondering how long it had been since he felt her walls close in around his muscle. It wasn't like the sexual energy wasn't there it was, only thing Dawayne and Serenity could feel those feelings raging from within. They didn't pounce on each other like the wild sex creatures, they were when they were together. He unlocked his car and crawled in, turned the ignition and sat back in his seat. He didn't know why he was so exhausted, he thought of Serenity. Wondering what she was doing, wondering if she was thinking of him. Dawayne opened his eyes, and sat up turned up the music popped it in reverse. By the time Dawayne got home, it was dark and the roads were wet from all the rain. He pulled into his parking space, walked up the stairs and began his nightly ritual. Laying his head down on his pillow, he replayed the conversation they had that evening. The same scenario kept happening, they weren't doing anything bad they were just talking to each other. It had to be sign Dawayne thought, how you could have a dream and repeat that dream. While dreaming that dream numerous times with the result being exactly the same. In a few short weeks he would be able get off work and go to her place, even better if he got off work and she was waiting for him at home. Buzz, Buzz Dawayne's phone went off. He looked at the time in the right hand corner, it illuminated 11:20pm

Hewooo
If you're awake
You should be sleeping
Because you got to work in the morning
But anyways
Wynter and will be taking a holiday in two weeks

Do you think you could pay for the room?
Neither of us have a credit card
Only Debit
We'll pay you back

He replied back and rolled over and feel asleep. He woke up that morning with inspiration, he wanted her to know how much he loved her. He was going to be able to spend a holiday with her, not just an hour, the whole fucking thing.

SHHHHHH SHE'S
IN THE ROOM

The work week came to an end for Dawayne, and he was going to spend a weekend holiday with Serenity. Even though Wynter was going to be there too, he could give two fucks. His phone chimed, he looked at the message.

**We just got in town
Heading to motel right now
So meet up with us in like thirty minutes
Staying at the Seaside Lodge**

Dawayne was excited, that morning he had made up some enchiladas to take to their room. He knew they would be a lil hungry and knew that Serenity loved enchiladas. He got his backpack and food and headed out the door. He was so excited, so alive. This was going to be the first time in weeks that he was going to spend some good quality time with Serenity. Hell he was just glad he was going to spend a whole fucking day with her, and possibly spend the night. Dawayne showed up at the Seaside Lodge, texted Serenity to see what room they were in. He found a spot to park in, got his gear and food and headed to their room. He knocked on the door and was welcomed with a huge ass huge from Serenity." I can't believe this is happening, like this is going to be the best day ever!" He walked into the room, and saw Wynter he said hello and then found a place to sit. Wynter was getting ready for the day, and Serenity was figuring out what she was going to wear. "Guess what I brought?" Dawayne said. "Enchiladas!" Serenity asked. She looked at him with a no you didn't look, "It's hard to surprise you if we can connect on that level of you know what I made." He pulled out some paper plates and plastic forks. It was still warm, he pulled it out of the oven before he left the house. They got down on them enchiladas, they watched a lil bit of television. "Let's go on an adventure," Serenity said to both Wynter and Dawayne. Well what is it you want to do, there is so much that can be done."" The scene during the day is nothing to brag about, but during the night the possibilities are endless." He had an idea, they left and headed out for an adventure. They arrived at a park, the two played and reminisced while Dawayne watched and laughed. Dawayne heard a bell in the distance, it was a man selling gelato. Dawayne walked to the man and asked what he was selling, "I'll take two of those and that one."

Gave the man his money and a lil extra for tip, Wynter and Serenity hit the swings and laughed and told stories of their childhood while enjoying their cool frozen treat. It was a lil warm so Dawayne asked them if they wanted to go on another adventure. He headed across town and headed to the byway listening to, Blink-182, and Sublime. When he got to the byway he pulled over and told Serenity to take over, she had never driven on the byway and today he was feeling good. He gave her a pep talk, and told her that he wasn't going to let anything bad happen to them while she was behind the wheel. He got out the car and went to the passenger side, he had to reassure her that she had this. He told her to get out of the car, "I want you to have this experience." Driving on the byway during the fall was one of the missed beauties they had in the area. Wynter was in the back seat laughing to herself, "If you don't get in the driver seat I will," she said. Dawayne and Wynter laughed, Serenity pushed Dawayne out the way and went to the driver side. She took a deep breath before she sat down behind the wheel, she adjusted the mirrors and found the right spot in seating. She looked in the rear view mirror and saw a car coming, she waited even though the car was about a quarter mile away. She waited for the car to pass, she put the car into drive and turned the wheel. Another car was heading their way, she paused again waiting for this car to pass. This happened about two more times and then Dawayne said," There is nobody coming behind us or in front of us, you got this, and I got you!" She pulled onto the byway and they were off, they were off to a slow start but Serenity found her groove and they were good. While Serenity focused on the road, Wynter and Dawayne talked about music. Realizing they had a few things in common as well, Wynter was a very attractive black woman. It was hard for him not to think of the possibilities of the evening. They laughed, told stories, Serenity about to get on the autobahn and Dawayne stopped her. He told her to pull over and he would take it from there. She had done well and surprised herself the byway was not as bad as she had made it out to be. Serenity wanted to get lit, and Wynter was on the same page. Serenity wanted that STICKY, and Wynter wanted that Yeager. Dawayne pulled into to his parking space at his place, told the ladies he was going to get a hold of his homie, and get some Yeager. He got a hold of his homie, and he told him it be about fifteen minutes.

So while Dawayne waited he went to get the Yeager, by the time he paid for that fifteen minutes had passed and he was on his way to his homies. He got that sticky and headed back to his place, he came back and the two black queens where listening to music and talking. He showed Wynter the bottle of Yeager, and Serenity the sticky. "We going to get fucked up," Serenity said. "I'm not drinking that big ass bottle," Wynter said. "Hey I' 'will match whatever you drink, drink for drink, so it doesn't seem like you the only one getting lit." "Got yourself a deal," Wynter said. They all climbed in the car heading to the Seaside Lodge, by the time they made it to the room it was dark and almost 9:00pm. They warmed up the enchiladas and eat dinner, while eating they watched music videos. For some reason Wynter was stuck on Stevie Stone's," Lets gets fucked up." They watched that video on repeat most of the night," There is Serenity," Wynter said as a drunken friend had to be helped up from the party in the music video. They laughed and watched more videos, Dawayne prepared the sticky and they stepped out the room. The scene was crazy outside the room, there was a birthday party going on at the pool, and some guys were smoking vape next to them. One of the guys asked if they wanted a hit," No thanks," Dawayne said to the guy.

As he said no thanks the guy took a big hit and created a dragon cloud, covering his friend in the walk way. They took a couple hits of the sticky and saved the rest for later. In no time they had the munchies, so they walked to the nearest store. They got their favorite treats while they shopped.

Smart Pop White Cheddar Popcorn
Haribro Gummy Worms
Jerky
Skittles
Sprite
Some other cold beverage
Some chocolate candy

They paid for their snacks and headed back to the room. Wynter used her key card and they were back in the room. They put back on music videos and ate their munchies, and found themselves watching let's get fucked up again by Stevie Stone. They all looked at each other and started laughing, Dawayne asked Wynter if she was ready for another shot. She moved closer to him and he was ready to pour her the whole damn bottle, and see what she was like FUCKED UP!! Wynter took a sip out the bottle, then she took another swig." All right then," Dawayne said and with that he took two drinks. They watched some more videos, than the Serenity decided to turn on Spring Breakers. While the movie was starting Wynter was in the bathroom getting cleaned up for the night, in Dawayne's head he was waiting for her to come out wearing some sexy ass black lingerie. Asking when the party was going to start, and then he would be done. TKO both black beauties and a night to sure remember for the rest for his life. Serenity pounced on him like a lioness trying to feed her cubs, they made out for a bit. Dawayne couldn't keep his hands to himself. His fingers wondered to her outer walls, she was wet like a slip n slide. He teased her a bit and then Wynter would poke her head out and see what was going on. If she wanted to see a show he would let her watch he thought, and if she wanted to join that would be even better. The sexual pulse in the room was strong and energy was thick. He wasn't sure if Serenity was thinking the same things as him, and if she was then they should've went for it. Wynter came out the bathroom, not in sexy lingerie, but sweats and a T. It was still sexy to him, she laid on the bed and chuckled to herself like she knew what was going on in the room before she came out. As Dawayne and Serenity played around on the other bed shit started getting to hot, he put his finger inside her sweetness. He started working his magic, and she was falling under his spell. Wynter rolled over, and then Serenity took flight. Dawayne was taking her on a ride, and a wet one for sure. He felt the balloon inside her walls swell up, and he attacked with rapid movement of his finger. Serenity moaned and couldn't control herself he had taken control. " Shhh she is in the room," Dawayne said. She squirted soaking the comforter and her black boy shorts, his favorite.

"I don't give a FUCK," Serenity said. That's all it took and Dawayne went to the television turned it off, muscle full erect and red sexual energy on overload he undressed.

Dawayne slid into the bed quietly, and Serenity climbed on top. She took her hand s and grabbed his, guiding him on a personal tour of her body. She led him to her breast, petite yet able to hold in his hands, she guided him down her side. She teased herself by allowing him to graze her outer walls and folds. His warmth, his energy made her sweetness tingle. Her walls on the inside started to extract her sweet nectar, Dawayne could feel the wetness with his finger. He wanted to taste her, pull her folds into his mouth and suck and nibble until she tapped out. He gripped her ass in his hands and squeezed, while pulling her closer to him. She attacked his neck, and started biting and sucking. He pulled her in closer, it aroused him the pain the pleasure the mixture of the two. Serenity was trying to get him to yell or scream, he stayed in the zone. The pain became pleasure and he could not feel any longer, the creature with had woke. Serenity placed her hands on his muscle and began stroking, asking if he liked the technique she had. She was rough but it felt fucking amazing, he liked it rough and when she slid her sweetness over the top of it he almost lost his mind. He wasn't expecting her to tease him, she teased him a while. While this was all going on Wynter was still in the room, tossing and turning. Dawayne was sure she was still awake, and trying to cover the sexual sounds coming from the bed beside her. Dawayne thought if she said something he was just going to ask her if she wanted to join. Wynter rolled over and said," What the fuck you two, really?" Dawayne said, "You know you could always join." Wynter looked at Dawayne then Serenity, she moved out of her bed and into theirs. Dawayne looked at Wynter and said," You sure you down, like down." She then took Serenity's hands and moved them from his muscle. She then pulled her hair back and began sucking him, her mouth unfamiliar and new. He laid back, and Serenity moved above his head and sat on his face. Placing her sweet nectar onto his lips, Wynter continued stroking and sucking his muscle. Dawayne wanted Serenity to turn around so she could face Wynter. He lifted her up and flipped her over, she was now facing Wynter. Serenity saw Wynter stroking his muscle and got jealous, she took over showing her how he liked it. He wanted to explore Wynter, he sat up and pushed her back down so he could see her tunnel. He hiked her ass up and slid himself into her tight dark tunnel. While he was putting in work, Serenity repositioned herself to be facing Wynter again. She looked Dawayne straight in the eyes, and gave him the nod.

Serenity then rammed her sweetness into Wynter's face, at the same time Dawayne pulled out just leaving the tip still in the dark. Thrusting his muscle the same time Serenity rammed her sweetness in her best friends face. Wynter growled like a breast feeding off her prey, the crazy thing was that she was the prey.

Serenity and Dawayne were the predators, and they were

going to feed off her as if she was the fountain of youth. Wynter devoured her best friends pussy, Serenity was surprised of the hunger she had for her sweetness. She wanted to pay the favor in return. Dawayne opened his eyes, and saw Serenity looking at him like he ate her skittles. She pulled on his muscle and slid it into her dripping wet sweetness, he looked for Wynter she was still laying in the other bed all covered up. "Holy Bobby Brown, what the fuck that was crazy." Serenity looked at him and just smiled, like she knew what he was thinking. He had lightning flash daydream, he came back to reality and focused his attention on Serenity. That night Dawayne became a wizard, he found a new spell with his fingers and his muscle. They fucked for the rest of that night, the morning came a knocking. His phone went off, just his alarm. Waking him up from an amazing dream, the day that he had spent with Serenity was one to remember. The night was even better, the day dream he had was fucked up and amazing at the same time. Dawayne crawled out the bed looking for his clothes, while trying to be stealth like a ninja. He laughed cause once Serenity got him going last night, being quite was the last thing on his mind. Thinking all the sounds that Serenity had made that night, if that didn't wake up Wynter she was a dead sleeper. If she heard them in the act, she was a good actress. He found his clothes, and dressed. Shirt on backwards he fixed himself, Serenity got up from the bed. Her naked silhouette sat up from the bed and slowly stood up. Dawayne put his arms around her so tight, she held on to him like she was never going to see him again. Kissing her and whispering that he loved her, she pulled him in closer. "I don't want you to leave," "I don't want to leave, I wish I could stay here till you leave." They stood there quietly, body to body thinking how much they were going to miss each other to themselves. His alarm went off again it was time to leave his queen, he was going to see her soon any ways. It was just torture having to leave her after spending the night with her. He grabbed his backpack and things and kissed Serenity one the lips then on the forehead." I love you, sleep with the dragons he said."

He was out the door, closing it quietly behind him. His eyes started to water, and a tear trickled down his cheek. He tried to hold the emotion in, he did his best but once he got to his car he cried. Leaving her was the hardest thing he had done in a while, he wanted to call in sick that day. Wanting to go run back to the room and crawl into the bed with her, he turned the ignition and drove towards the autobahn.

AMBITIONS
OF A RIDER

After that night spent with Dawayne, serenity found her ambition, realizing that she wanted to wake up every morning next to him. Serenity hit the books, and put in work on campus. She told Dawayne that she was looking to be finished there on campus by the end of December. That was only two weeks away, she was looking and apply for jobs everywhere that she could think. She wanted to be near him, looking at housing was a lil scary but she found a room in the middle of town. One morning Serenity came into the kitchen and surprised Dawayne, nobody even seen her come in. He told the staff that he had to go downstairs to get some supplies. He told Serenity to follow him, the snuck off without being seen or heard. Dawayne grabbed Serenity, lifted her off the ground and kissed her. She wrapped her legs around his waist, and the basement filled up with blue and red sexual energy. He held her there like that, squeezing on her plump round ass, and having the taste of her lips on his tongue. He pulled her dress up and caressed her thighs and butt in his hand. He couldn't help himself from having a finger graze upon her outer fold. It was warm and very wet, with just a flick of his thumb the sweet nectar of Serenity was saturating his thumb. He bent her over, hands going to her breast for a gentle squeeze. Moving to the nipples so hard and erect, his fingers did a ballet down her sides and to her sweetness. She stayed bent over and tried to hold the energy inside, his finger moved and glided along her walls as if he was playing lead violin in the New York Symphony. Dawayne put his fingers to work as if he had a solo and everyone in his life and him were dependent on him to make her come. He could tell she was about to come, her balloon was filled up and it was time for the water works. His fingers continued to work their magic, he could feel the walls contracting. The temperature started to rise, wet became wetter, and wetter began to slowly flood. A voice from above called out his name, his finger came to a dead stop. Stopping and listening for his name again, nothing maybe it was his old friend PARANIOA. Serenity pulled her dress down and tried to find a place to hide, there was silence from up above. Dawayne waited for what seemed like forever, those few seconds went by like pouring molasses.

His fingers slowly began to dance against her walls again." I'm like really wet down there, like trickling down my leg wet," Serenity whispered. He had to start slow, he could tell her walls were swollen and sensitive to the slightest touch.

He could feel the thick wet nectar on the tip of his finger, so sticky, so wet. Dawayne wanted to take her right there, he unbuckled his belt, unzipped his pants. Pulling out his muscle he slid himself along he folds, he could've slid right in but he liked teasing her. Teasing her folds, making her sweetness salivate for his muscle. Her sweetness trickled he could feel the warm wet nectar with the tip of his muscle. His muscle knocked on the door of her sweetness, just as he did that he heard his name being called again. "I guess that's a sign, if it's meant to happen it will happen." Serenity always had some smart shit to say, sex was in motion and they had to come to an abrupt stop right before climax. It didn't happen very often but when she felt it wasn't the right time, every time she was right. Each one of those times, if they began to fuck they would've been seen or caught. Serenity pulled down her dress, pulled Dawayne in for a kiss and snuck out the back. Dawayne got himself together, grabbed a couple items off the racks and headed up the stairs. He walked into one of the cooks on his way up the stairs, "We've been calling for you past fifteen minutes, and the freezer is locked." He went to the freezer and unlocked it. The rest of the day his head was up in the clouds, and his heart was jammed full of love. After work he went home did his nightly routine, and feel asleep with dreams of Serenity in his head. The remaining days until her departure, they soaked up as much taboo sexual sessions as possible. How different was it going to be after she was done with school? Dawayne was sure that this was real and not a damn thing was going to change what they had, or what they had created. To Dawayne this was one crazy moment, every moment with Serenity was like a newborn catching his or her first breath in the new world. These moments would continue he said to himself, the moments would only get better, more erotic, and more passionate. He was going to have that, have that feeling every night that the woman he was with was the one. The one he was going to marry, do things right, no mistakes, no second chances.

One night after dinner Serenity told him that she had a surprise, she had an interview the following morning. Dawayne was so excited and proud of her, again he asked her." You're doing this because you want to?"

"Don't do this because you think this is what I want, I want the best for you either here or there and that's what matters." Serenity told him that she was doing it because she wanted to, Dawayne was fine with her answer.

On the day of graduation, her family was there and he could only think. One day I'm going to meet and their going to be thinking where have they seen him before. He would play it off and say he has one of those faces. He went back to thinking about the new moments he would create with his one and only, his Nubian Queen, his caramel praline.

That day was the beginning of Elecuphoria, the foundation had been built with letters and notes. Trust and honoring someone, that's what they had built while at their taboo sessions they had all over the campus. No more having to worry if they were going to be caught, they were on the outs. Hiding was no longer a thought, he was hers and she was his. She moved into her loft that had an amazing view of the city. She had a lot to take care of, and many things to get for her new place. Dawayne couldn't wait to get off of work so that he could see her, to taste her, feel her next to him. To hold her for as long as she permitted, or until he feel asleep or vice versa.

BEHIND CLOSED
DOORS

Make It Easy, by Ne-Yo played in the back ground as Dawayne cleaned his apartment. He was in hog heaven, his Queen was in hopefully all warm and cozy in her studio apartment. Dawayne had took a vacation, the first vacation he had took in a long ass time. He wanted to spend every moment possible with Serenity, and that's what they did. He took a few things in his bag and headed over to Serenity's place, it felt weird saying that Serenity's place. Dawayne laughed to himself, thinking how far they've come. From a few words on a piece of paper, to creating amazing moments together, and now finally her being here. He received the call from her and he was on his way, as he drove the autobahn he thought of moments that they were going to create now. He knew there would be some ups and downs, that's normal in any relationship. Thinking that this was not a relationship though, they always agreed on the word moment. The definition of moment was a very brief period of time, that's why their saying live in the moment was so them. They never knew when the moment would end, enjoying every second of every moment. Etched into both of their flesh, they could always look at their tattoos. Live in the moment would be a motto that they would live by, enjoy each moment with Serenity as if it was your last. He turned up the music in his car, checking for you, by R. City he jammed out to that song. Singing as if Serenity could hear him. He went through the roundabout and headed downtown. Fall was in the air, Serenity's favorite season LOVE was in the air as well it couldn't be prevented. Serenity was so excited to see him she jumped into his arms. He gave her the biggest hug, which followed with a kiss. "I can't believe this," Serenity said. Dawayne just held her and didn't want to let go, he agreed with a soft whisper. She had to show him her studio apartment, she lead him into the flat. The place was decent, it wasn't the best and wasn't the worst. Kind of in the middle, she had a fridge a sink, a pantry. He knew that Serenity loved him, he loved her back with more than she would ever know. He appreciated her for what she did and all she was going to do. She had her bag ready and they headed out the lil room. It was time to go on an adventure, time to make some more moments. They got in the car and headed off. They arrived at his place a few hours later, they headed up the stairs and Dawayne unlocked the door. The sexual energy was strong, it engulfed both of them as they entered the apartment.

It didn't take very long for Serenity to be naked, Dawayne pulled her pants down and revealed her sweetness. It was as if it had been hidden and locked away and he had to go through a mission. Being successful in the mission he was able to have the best prize ever. He put his head on her stomach and started kissing. His lips always seemed to find spots that were sensitive and ticklish. She giggled and re-positioned on the couch, Dawayne pulled her in closer. His tongue began to slowly warm her folds, he spit on her sweetness. Placing his tongue deep in her walls, he flicked his tongue up and down. With a swirl their and a flick their it was as if he was signing his John Hancock on her warm wet walls with his tongue. If his tongue was spray paint, he would have created the most amazing piece of graffiti. His tongue was strong and conditioned to work hours if needed, to get her to orgasm or even better squirt. Serenity grabbed a pillow and cover her face, to hide her facial expressions and her moans. Dawayne grabbed the pillow and threw it across the room, "I want you to let it out, and don't hold that shit in." Dawayne whispered in her ear, he calmed her down and grabbed a condom. He eased his muscle into her walls, she exhaled like it was her first time. He was gentle as if it was her first time, but he would hold back the sexual creature for as long as he could. Her walls were so constricted, like a python crushing its prey. Her folds were warm and wet like an undiscovered underground cave, he glided in her sweetness smooth. As if his muscle was built for her sweetness, her walls would always take him as if they were built for only him. He pulled himself out, slowly just sliding the tip in, he would move with his own rhythm and it would make Serenity go crazy. She hated that he would tease her like that, just the tip felt so fucking good, so god damn good. Serenity enjoyed it but would never say that she did, but the expression and sounds she made. Let him know that he was on to something great, onto something wet and gushing. They moved from the couch to his kitchen, he had her bent over on the counter, from behind it was as if the sweetness was devouring his muscle. The constriction felt good, the wetness and most made him lose it. He thought to himself you better not fucking do it, don't you fucking come right now. He pulled himself out of her juicy, dripping walls, he got down on his knees and started licking the nectar that was coated on her outer walls. She had come already, but he had more for her. Hell more if he could, he would last the rest of the day and go into the late hours of the evening. That is exactly what happened, he put his finger in his mouth and licked it. Moving his finger along the edges of her walls, he got the lil bit of nectar that he was unable to lick up with his tongue. Scooping it up with his finger, he placed her nectar into his mouth. So sweet so warm, the creamy elixir set his mouth on a mystical trip. The elixir of Serenity's sweetness would be all that he would need to survive. He eased his finger into her sweetness, and slowly filled her balloon up. She moaned and screamed out to the god's or anybody that would listen. She found her inner Mariah Carey, when she hit her falsetto her stomach twitched. Dawayne could feel her balloon was about to burst, he speed up his repetition. She tried to grab a hold of anything that would allow, she gripped the countertop the breakfast bar. She went for him and he pushed her back gently, she laid back with hesitation. He eased her down, she was going to squirt, he could feel it, and she felt that she had to pee. "That's what it feel like, just let it happen, I want you to fucking squirt," Dawayne said quietly. He pulled her long legs around his waist and carried her into his room. He laid her on the bed, and she ran into the bathroom. He heard her lift he lid then sit down, while she tried to squeeze a drop of pee out he got on his MacBook and opened a playlist.

Not any playlist their playlist, they had many on his laptop, but this was the one that had every song they agreed upon for a special moment shared with each other. Sexual or non-sexual he clicked the play icon, and as he did Ryan Leslie Addicted boomed through the speakers. Serenity opened the bathroom door," I guess I didn't have to pee, She said. "I knew you didn't have to pee, you literally went to the bathroom before we started. "She looked at him and smiled while saying should a, could a, would a. Then she jumped onto the bed and laughed, Dawayne took a deep breath the SAVAGE was knocking on his door. He could take advantage of her unawareness and attack the sweetness like a stealthy assassin, or he could just let her gloat and think she was the shit. As she jumped onto the bed and tried to roll he caught her in mid flip, he got her legs held them and slid his tongue into her sweetness. It was hot, and sticky, he gently grazed on her folds and then moved into her walls. She was still full and he knew that he could make her squirt. He started pumping up the balloon with his finger again, "I want you inside of me," she whispered. He acted like he didn't hear what she said," what did you say," He asked, "I want you inside of me," she said louder.

He pulled on another condom, tossing the golden wrapper across the room. Dawayne slid his muscle along the length of her folds, guiding himself inside her walls. She was already sensitive, and her balloon was full and ready the nectar was ready to be tapped into. He took his tongue and lips and moved along the curves and crevices of her body. He worked his way from between her slender long beautiful thighs, and kissed where her pelvic and thigh meet. Dawayne opened his mouth as wide as he could, engulfing all the flesh he could, she moaned and arched her back. Biting her lip, closing her eyes she was transported to ELECUPHORIA, it was their place their KINGDOM. A place where a King and his Queen could let out their inner sexual creatures. Just be themselves, just be two energies scientifically and chemically right for each other. He continued to move along the length of her body, moving to her ear lobes. Caressing her lower lobe with his bottom lip, as his lips closed in on her ear. The heat from his mouth and tongue sent a tingle from her ear all the way to her toes. Dawayne's tongue did a contemporary dance on the stage that was Serenity's body. His tongue moving like it had never done before, his tongue didn't get tired as it moved every inch of her body. His tongue came to a dead stop at his favorite feature, the legs. He began to kiss and suck on her thighs, swirling his tongue in between kisses. He planted his body between her thighs, he used his shoulders to push her thighs out. Wrapping his arms under her thighs and holding her hips down, he slid his tongue into her sweetness. Dawayne's tongue moved constant as if it were to stop, his tongue would fall out of his mouth.

"Oh my God, oh my fucking God," Serenity called out. As Dawayne worked his tongue, she tried to get way but the way he had her pinned down that wasn't going to happen today. He knew that she would try to get away, that was always part of the act. She would be ready to come, and then she would slither out of the bed. Sometimes she wouldn't make it off the bed, she would be half way on the bed, screaming out to the gods. Dawayne would pull some NIGGA shit, no matter what way Serenity tried to run from her screaming orgasm he would get her. Dawayne pulled Serenity by the arm, making her flip over to her belly. He slapped her ass, "Is that all you got," she said like a smart ass. Dawayne cocked his hand back, *SMACK, SLAP, WHAMP.* "For real is that the hardest you can slap," He cocked his hand back again. Trying to deliver pleasure and a lil bit of pain, his hand hit flesh.

Serenity moaned putting her face down looking for a pillow, as her face went down her plump juicy now red ass was in the air. Looking down seeing red marks on her caramel skin, a large hand print was slightly visible. Dawayne grabbed onto her hips, she sat right into him. Guiding his muscle with one hand and holding on to her waist with another he entered. "Ohhh, Ohhh," She pleaded. "Is that too much he whispered?" She nodded he eased some of his muscle out of her warm walls, the rest of him felt naked. He grabbed her by the shoulders, pulling her in close. He took her arms and moved to her hands, he pulled her arms to her side as he thrusted his muscle. Serenity tried to keep her composure, this was not the time nor the day. The SAVAGE was in control and once it was in control there was no holding back. Serenity screamed and screamed with pleasure, blurting out words that she had no control over. The way he moved his muscle inside of her, had a rhythm there was something with his rhythm that caused her to have an extreme case of Tourette's. She lost her breath, lost her ability to speak, and then she came. She came with vengeance, there was too much force when she came. Natural juices and nectars forced him as she growled. She sprayed and dripped all over the bed, he body trembled went into convulsions. Her head up against the wall, and shoulder as well, Serenity wasn't able to get away. From the foot of the bed to the head of the bed, the sex was so intense that the covers were pulled off the bed. The comforter was balled up at the foot of the bed, the fitted sheet was hanging on for dear life. Dawayne let Serenity catch her breath, she ran into the dining room to get her inhaler. She took a couple hits off her inhaler as she walked back to the room.

When she came back he said, "You didn't tap out, you have to tap out that's the only way I'll know to stop!" Serenity replied back, "Who said I wanted you to stop?" Dawayne took a mental picture of Serenity standing there so naked, so beautiful, he wanted more of her. His hunger for her was at peak, Serenity jumped into the bed and she began to play around with him. A conversation about the future popped up, and the two were lost in the moment. It was only moments later when Serenity started messing with him in that way she always would when she was ready for another round. Dawayne played along, and let her do her thing. She started kissing him then she covered herself with the comforter and headed down south. Serenity placed her hands on his muscle, rubbing him stroking him, making his muscle flex and show its true strength.

As he became erect she placed her soft lips on the tip of his muscle and gave it a kiss. He then heard her spit, he could feel the warmth of spit coat his muscle. She took his muscle into her mouth and began her mission, she had done her homework. He had her watch his favorite porn star, Bonnie Rotten. She had the proper technique, she could show any woman how to suck a dick the right fucking way. He could tell she did her homework, her technique was on point. Spit, loads of fucking spit, and long and aggressive strokes. "You like that," Serenity asked. Dawayne nodded like she was able to see him, he had forgot that she was under the comforter. He answered back with a," Fuck yea, God that fucking feels AMAZING!" He had never received head the way he ever wanted, others would not have any interest or do the same lousy ass blow job. Dawayne thought that it was only right to take time and enjoy a women's natural vitamins for as long as he could, or for as long as she could handle it until she pleaded for him to give them the D. He only expected the same in return, Serenity was the first. The first to take his advice, to take the homework and study the art and techniques Bonnie could teach her. Hell teach any woman, he always thought communication was the key. Sexual communication, like the way he learned from Savannah. She guided him and told him the dos and don'ts. The person you are sexually open with should be willing to go the distance, to do the homework to bring your sexual experience to a whole new level. Serenity was a quick learner, she spit on his muscle stroking him aggressively and fast. "I want you to come for me, I want you to come on my tits." Serenity pleaded for him to come on her tits. "I want you on top of me first," he said. "I want to feel you wrapped around me, then I will do whatever you want me to." Serenity hesitated, riding was not her specialty, nor did she have much experience in the art of riding. "Just take it slow, you are in control, you control the speed, you control how deep it goes." Serenity climbed on top, her warm thighs rubbed against his. He reached for his muscle and she diverted his hand away, she grabbed it with gentle hands and rubbed the tip with her thumb. It was still wet and coated with her spit, she sat up and pulled his muscle towards her outer folds. He caught her for a slight second teasing herself, as he would always would do to her. She pulled herself up and relaxed her body and mind, sliding his muscle into her deep sweet folds. She eased his muscle an inch at a time, on her own accord.

She was in control, she could take it as deep as she wanted or ride him as if she was trying to BREAK a horse. Her body quivered as she took him in deeper, she sat up high preventing all of his muscle to go deep inside her walls. Dawayne grabbed her by the hips, enjoyed the rarity of being rode as if he was an animal. Serenity found her spot, the spot that hit all nerve endings. Drunk in Love, by Beyoncé ran through his head. She was riding on his surfboard," graining on that wood, graining, graining on that wood." Serenity was in charge, but Dawayne couldn't take it anymore. Her speed and penetration were amazing, he just wanted it all. His red sexual energy took over the room, the SAVAGE took over. He grabbed Serenity by the hips, and rose his hips. Giving her all of him she gasped, he started slow and deep. Then her walls constricted his muscle, taking him to a place he had never been. Dawayne lifted his body off of the bed, raising his hips Serenity had no choice but to go along for the ride. He thrust became quick and smooth, she had no place to put her arms. She tried to cover her eyes and hide her facial expressions of straight euphoria, that didn't work. She tried to scream out to the heavens, no one answered. She grabbed onto his thighs and dug her nails into the flesh of his thighs. The pain only made Dawayne go harder and faster, the pain turned into pleasure. The Savage was in complete control, Serenity started reaching for anything that she could hold onto. Pulling the cover off the bed, grabbing pillows, whatever she grabbed Dawayne tossed, or she lost control and ended up dropping any ways. "Holy fucking shit, Oh my Fucking God, fuck me, fuck me, she screamed." Sweat beads glistened off Serenity's brow, sweat trickled from her chest to her stomach. Her stomach contacted as if she was giving birth to a love child. The sweat tickled down her abs and to her sweetness, the sound of nectar and honey colliding between two bodies echoed in the room. He kept his position and keep his speed, Serenity pleaded for him to stop. "I can't, I can't, and you have to come for me first." A sound came out of Serenity that had been rumbling from the deepest corners of her sexual goddess. When she made that sound he could feel her walls caving in, her body became weak. Serenity found some way to put together all of her energy and place her hand on the bed to tap out, she hit the bed three times.

"I tap out, I tap out," she said, with sweat beads glistening all over her body. Dawayne knew the rules, he slowly lowered Serenity and himself out of the air and found sanctuary in the mattress. Serenity was out of breath, she was scrambling to find her inhaler. She found it on the floor, she took a deep breath as the medication touched her lungs. It was not enough, she took another deep breath in taking the medicine, her lungs ached and her sweetness cried and trickled down her leg. She was out of breath, out of energy, her body was physically drained. Dawayne put in work on her walls, her folds, he got up and went to the fridge and got two frosted cups out of the freezer. Placing them on the counter, getting the bottle of cold ass water out of his fridge, he filled the two cups. He drank his water in seconds, refilled it, drank it all, and refilled it one last time. Took a lil sip and then headed to his room, Serenity laid there tired and worn. Handing her the glass she took a drink," Fuck man, fuck, I have never had that feeling in my life before." Dawayne wasn't sure what she meant so he asked, "Was it at least a good feeling?" Serenity looked at him and said," I feel like I was just taken off the planet, out of or solar system, taken to a new place." Dawayne popped off, "That's what we call Elecuphoria, a place we both have to enjoy and explore together." Dawayne explained the feeling of being completely free with your body, sexually, emotionally, mentally, physically, then you will know what the sexual experience should feel like. "Now you know what it feels like, know you know the endurance you have to have to experience it." They laid there naked talking for a while, then they feel asleep.

Elecuphoria- *A place created by a single pair sexual energies, when two people are on all levels of the sexual experience. They are found to be taken to a place out of this world, although this place drains you from your energy. It also creates the chemicals in your brain to make your body feel Euphoric.*

Dawayne woke up before Serenity, he laid their and stared at her for a brief moment. He got up and looked around for his underwear, he couldn't find them. So he just decided to grab another pair from his closet. He walked into his living room, looked for the remote and turned the television on. He sat down and covered up with a blanket that was on his couch, he heard a sound. He turned and looked, it wasn't Serenity how he wanted her to be awake. To be engulfed with all her positive blue energy, his eyes went back to the television. Some late night crap they play in between good shows, to fill the television slots. Dawayne heard the toilet flush and he knew that she was awake, his heart filled with warmth. She walked into the living room in just a T-shirt, the blood to his muscle began to flow to his tip. She snuggled all close to him, and covered herself with the blanket that he was using. He had only half his body covered, and she was all warm and cozy. He knew from that action, that she was ready for round two. She would do that, fuck with him. It was her way of flirting, he could tell when she was ready for more. Even though she had no idea, what she was getting herself ready for. They sat there and cuddled for a while then the sexual advances began, serenity slowly slithered her foot near his muscle. Moving her foot in a way that, caused more blood to flow to the tip. He looked at her,

"What?" Serenity said as innocent as toddlers first spoken sorry. "You know what you're getting yourself into?" Serenity again moved her foot along the length of his muscle, starting from shaft to tip. The warmth started from his shaft, as he became more aroused, his muscle grew its full capability. She massaged her feet over his muscle, slowly becoming more aroused herself. She stood up from the couch and then stood right in front of him. She sat down slow as if she was giving him a lil show, her hips whined left to right. Her arms straight, wrist bent, hands gripping his thigh. Serenity dropped it on him slow, and then picked it back up. She only did this once, the muscle trapped in the briefs wanted out. Dawayne reached for Serenity's hips, whining her from side to side slow. Serenity threw it back on him, pushing her as to his stomach. He could feel when her ass was sliding over him, as she pushed it back he could feel the warmth. The warmth was hiding behind some warm sweet nectar. His muscle so sensitive, so hard, he could feel her folds. Like a high-definition metal detector, his muscle could popped through.

Somehow it was able to break free and find a way out of his briefs, right into her sweetness. She had teased him, and in doing so life said," Not today, it's not going your way today!" The tip of his muscle slid along the outer folds of her sweetness. She sat up, Dawayne put his hands on her hips, pulling in he kissed her butt cheek. He gave the other cheek the same attention and then he attempted to take a bite. Dawayne placed his mouth on her butt, he opened his mouth as wide as it could go. Then he sunk his mouth into her tender caramel flesh, he bit down. Serenity moaned, not sure for pain or pleasure. Dawayne bit down even harder, "You call that a bite. "Serenity said trying not to laugh, he bit down harder. She tensed up, he could tell that did a lil something to her. He had her, he grabbed her hips and grabbed her thong. Pulling them down so fast Serenity couldn't have changed the scenario if she could. She bent down as if she could get them back up and then Dawayne slipped a finger right in her sweetness. His finger moved straight to her spot, and her hands went straight to her thighs. "Stawwwwwwp," she said. He knew once the act was on there was no turning back. Serenity made the first move by rubbing her feet on his muscle. After that all she was doing was just waiting to see how long he could go with her teasing him. Soon as she dropped it on him, he already had his next move in progress. He was always two steps ahead of her, that's when he would pull some NIGGA shit on her. He moved his finger like he was casting a spell on her, she started stuttering. She was trying to get him to quit, but this was their game. Once it had been started by the other party, you could only end the session by tapping out. No safe words, no hand or body signals. Tapping out, placing the hand in front of the partner and tapping the surface twice. Dawayne was casting a spell on Serenity's sweetness, by whirling his finger past the folds and hit the WALL. Serenity pleaded for him to stop, as she rose her ass up higher. It was very visible that she was aroused, and when she hiked her ass up to hit that spot. He knew that he had her where he wanted her, thinking that she was in charge. She wasn't in charge, just because she hiked her ass up to get a deeper orgasm. Dawayne stopped moving his finger, Serenity clinched her body automatically. His finger danced as if he was the snake charmer and she was the cobra. "Don't you move, don't fucking move!" Dawayne heard being called to him. He did as she pleaded and then he saw that look in her eyes, she was up to something.

Slowly moving his finger again, against her walls he took over. Pulling her ass into his face he kissed her cheeks again. Sliding his tongue slowly and flicking the folds, up from her sweetness to her starfruit. His lips gently kissed each cheek very strategically, and gliding between the two cheeks he came upon an exotic fruit. Starfish, it was new unexplored territory he was working with. Dawayne traced the shape of the starfruit with his tongue, Serenity felt a new sensation intrigue her sexual senses. The edge of his tongue attempted to go inside this new territory,

it was sight every time he was successful. Serenity would moan and arch her back, forcing the tongue to penetrate the fruit even further. Rolling his tongue along these new edges, he became even more aroused. He gripped her hips, ran his fingers the length of her legs touching each nerve ending. His tongue went to the start fruit again, tracing the darkened outline with his tongue. Dawayne then stood up and traded positions, Serenity was on her knees bent over on the couch. With one swift movement he was in between her thighs, tasting her sweetness and praying to be sprayed or enjoy some sweet nectar. His hands moved up her sides, fingers sliding between each rib. He squeezed, pulling Serenity in closer she tried to say something. It had already started and slurred speech was the first sign. Moving his tongue along her folds, Serenity held her breath. Overcome with arousal and pleasure she growled," You aren't going to do shit!" Dawayne sat up behind her and slid his muscle into her walls, NIGGA shit. Serenity was breathless, as Dawayne swirled his hips as if he was mixing pancake batter with his muscle. "Oh my fucking god, yes, yes, yes, who's pussy is that." Dawayne smacked that ass, telling Serenity that it was his pussy. "Whose dick is that?" Dawayne asked Serenity, she didn't have an answer. Hell she could barely speak, the way he was moving inside of her. All of her energy was being used not to come right then and there, he was trying to make her come. Make her come long, and fucking hard. He grabbed onto her breast and squeezed, applying pressure all the way till he reached her nipple then he pinched slightly. Serenity's nipples were cold and hard, he wanted to suck on them. He pulled himself from her walls, from her folds. Flipping Serenity over he sucked on her sweetness for a second, then his tongue moved its way to her breast. Not before his tongue took the scenic route to her nipples, he left no stone unturned as he tasted her natural saltiness.

Serenity exhaled deeply as his tongue glided along her abs, he rerouted and found himself close to her folds again. Flicking his tongue on her folds to tease her. He jumped back to the untouched flesh his tongue had missed on the trip to the dark, hard, cold nipples. Sucked and kissed, mouthwatering as if he was eating a Palisade peach. Dawayne wanted more he sat up got on his knees, pulled Serenity close to him and began kissing her. Kissing her as if he knew today was the last day he would ever spend with her, her tongue came back with a tango of its own. She bit down and started sucking his top lip, the pain was real. He wanted to tap out already, she had a hold on his lip. Serenity wasn't holding back anything, she was going for the win. For the TKO, Dawayne could feel the blood being pinched off from his lip, his lip started to tingle. His lip went numb a few seconds later, once it went numb Dawayne didn't feel a damn thing. He pulled his lip back, as Serenity's teeth left a trail of dead skin behind. Dawayne's lip was swollen, and dark. Serenity had done damage, she was able to tag the beast. Leaving marks on Dawayne was hard to do, and when she was successful she had to find her sexual creature. She was like a vampire, her mouth was the most dangerous weapon she held. Dawayne pulled her in even more, he reached for a condom. Opening the package and placing it on his muscle like he had done it blindfolded, with one hand tied behind his back. It was on in seconds, and so was his stroke. Easing past her folds and being welcomed by her walls, she flexed. Letting him know that she knew that he was inside her, and that he wasn't being sneaky. Gliding between her folds his muscle kept a steady pace, he pulled up to show her that he was not being sneaky. That he had a condom on, he was just on that NIGGA shit, he was on that physical level. Completing the task of putting on a condom, with a quick and steady hand. She looked at him giving him the heads up, he proceeded. Taking his time to pass through her folds, he teased her. Just the tip, and super slow, the tip of his muscle flexed as it moved along the folds of her sweetness. He slid his muscle slowly from the start of her star fruit to the outer maybe more sensitive folds. Serenity quivered in excitement, he body got the chills. Goosebumps covered her moistened caramel flesh, Dawayne wrapped her legs around his waist and carried her to his bed. She placed her arms around his neck, kissing him, him kissing her. The passion meter was full, the sexual energy that was in the room was thick and heavy.

Red from him, blue from her, sexual energy may not be visible to the human eye. Yet Dawayne and Serenity's was strangely noticeable, the room would illuminate with the two energies and create a chemistry no scientist could ever match. Serenity fell on her back softly, Dawayne was right there. As she moved to find a better position, he kissed and sucked up her neck. His muscle was still nestled deep inside her sweetness, legs wrapped around his waist. Serenity's arms pressed up against the wall, and her energy being drained. She lost her battle with the wall, before she knew it her head was up against the wall. Head cocked to the side jammed up against the wall, with beads of sweat trickling down her collarbone. "Choke me!" Serenity said. Dawayne didn't hesitate, he got his hand and placed it on her throat. His hand was so huge, it nearly wrapped around her entire neck. As his hand went to her neck, she took one last breath. Dawayne gently placed his palm on the base of her neck, preventing any pressure points from being in his grasp. "Harder!" she gasped, he applied more pressure and her eyes began to water. As he was choking her, he slid in and out of her walls slowly. Putting all of his attention on her neck, the last thing he would want to do is make her pass out. Even though he had heard on talk radio that, orgasming right before you pass out is the most euphoric feeling sexually. He thought about it in his head, but he knew that he would have to talk to her about attempting to make her pass out. Serenity moaned, and cursed out to the gods the best she could, Dawayne's hands still around her neck. "Is that too much?" he asked. She growled out "Noooo," he asked her. "Harder?" she nodded and his grip tightened around her neck.

Dawayne could feel her as she swallowed, feel as she tried

to inhale the sexual energy in the air. Just as she took a deep breath in, she was filled with energy. Dawayne released his grip, Serenity gasped for air. He rolled over to allow Serenity room, she then pounced on him. She straddled him as if she was going to ride, she sat up on his dick and slid her folds down his muscle. Serenity twerk'd on his muscle for a lil bit, then she went in for the attack. Her sexual creature attacked his collarbone, mouth on his flesh she applied pressure. She bit down and sucked as hard as she could, then she moved the length from shoulder to shoulder. By the time she was done he had bite marks from shoulder to shoulder, he trusted himself deep inside her walls from the pleasure and the pain.

He had nowhere to go, he was under her control. "Mother fucker, son of a bitch, fuck, shit, fuck," he blurted out. The only thing he could do was try to run, and when he did so she would just bite down even harder. Trying to get away like a lil bitch had no choice, he got his arm. Waved it up and down, and tapped on the bed twice. Serenity rolled off him with the biggest smile, she knew she had won that match. Dawayne stumbled to his bathroom, he looked into the mirror. He saw his flesh had been tested on its toughness, he had perfect bite marks in the shape of two chains across his chest. "Damn you put some work on that, look I'm like 2 Chains." Dawayne laughed out loud, he had a sense of accomplishment all his own. He was no longer invincible, Serenity had been taken the win that ROUND. Dawayne crawled back into the bed with Serenity, "I think I've found my match." "I have never had anybody come close to making me tap out, and her you are all cute and shit." Dawayne told her how good it started to feel, and then he made it worse by trying to escape. When she bit down harder and he tried to scurry away, it only made it worse. "I had no choice, I had to tap out." "It felt as if blood was going to be trickling down my chest, and you pierced my flesh. "No other option then to TAP THE FUCK OUT."

THE ART OF
TAPPING OUT

During previous sexual sessions Dawayne and Serenity had, the tried safe words. They were fun and silly, but when they used them. There was no accomplishment felt, by hearing the safe word being yelled out. They agreed that they would only end a session of sex with only, and only a physical tap out. Two taps on any surface that was visible to the others eye. So when they had a whole day to fuck down the road, they both knew that in order to start a session you must get the other partner aroused. It was easy for serenity, all she had to do was put her energy on his muscle. Hovering her hand over his muscle as if she was putting a spell on him. Serenity was a lil different sometimes it could be a song, sometimes it could be his breath on her skin. The touch of his finger on her skin, his lips caressing nether reaches of his tongue. This is their first session, so they went over the rules plenty of times via text, email, or note and letter. One it was all said and done both parties made an agreement, to always follow the rules. Those were the rules, and they would follow them directly, if something changed they would agree on. In the beginning they used safe words, his was Watermelon.

Serenity's was Skittles, they found out shortly after a few sessions that safe words were too easy. You could get away from your partner and then say your safe word, tapping out was the right decision. There was personal achievement built by making your partner tap out.

FRENCH MAID
IN HIGH HEELS

One day Serenity made the plan that they would, eventually have to stay at her apartment. So they went to Dawayne apartment and he got his overnight stuff, and then they left for her place. They hit the autobahn in less than seven minutes, and they got to her place in less than thirty. Dawayne had to look for a parking place, there was parking available near Serenity's apartment. He wasn't sure that if he parked in any of those spots he would get towed. He decided to take the chance and parked it, they got their stuff and headed to her apartment. It was not too far from her building, and she was getting her keys out to open the main entrance to her building. They headed up the stairs and her place was right there on the second floor, soon as you get off her door was there. She opened the door and turned on the lights, her place was warm it smelled of sand wood chamomile. One of those plug in air fresheners," get comfortable." Serenity said, as he placed his stuff out of the way. She got her shower stuff, "What movie you want to watch?" Showing him his options of movies, he chose something that he had seen before. Serenity popped it into the dvd player and hit play," Watch this until I get back." He sat there on her futon, drinking some lemonade and watching the movie. What seemed like an hour later, Serenity turned the door knob and walked in. She was in her towel, she dried herself real slow. Knowing that she was teasing him the whole time, then she rubbed lotion all over her body. As she was doing this Dawayne became aroused, it was hard for him to hide his excitement. When she was done saturating her lovely caramel skin," I have a surprise for you, but you got to close your eyes." Shaking his head in agreement he closed his eyes," No peeking!" He could hear the sound of material, it wasn't for long. He could hear the material going up against something, not sure what it was he tried to peek." I said no peeking," Serenity growled at him. He heard footsteps sounding closer to him, she sat on his lap. Rubbing against his muscle, "Strap this for me!" Unsure of what was going on he attempted to do what she asked, with his eyes closed. Dawayne wasn't getting anywhere with that, "Just open your eyes to strap this, then close them once you have that finished." He did as he was told, and then he closed his eyes.

Think how hard that was strapping her up, with his eyes closed. He still didn't know what it was he was strapping up, he could hear her going throw a pile of something. He could hear thuds, something heavy and a lot feel onto the wooden floor. Thud, thud, he heard then he heard a quick movement. Then the sound of something rubbing up against something smooth. A loud thud, echoed in the apartment, another quick movement with the sound of smooth on smooth. Another loud thud, "Open your eyes!" Dawayne opened his eyes and their she stood, with black high heels wrapped around her lovely long fucking legs. With that a black and white French maid costume on, "Can I get you some more lemonade?" Serenity offered with a big smile on her face, she could tell Dawayne was still speechless. She had surprised him, words tried to come out of his mouth. He was staring at a Nubian Queen, her caramel skin shinned as the light in the room reflected of her freshly lotion flesh. His eyes were at her feet, he saw her calves flexed up because of her in high heels. He led his eyes on a slow adventure of the beauty that was in front of him. He had never had been on the side of being waited on, it was a lil different on this side. Handing her his glass she turned and took a few steps to the fridge, she opened the door and bent over slowly. He had seen he do this many times before, yet this time it was different. More exotic, more erotic, his eyes focused on her plump volleyball ass. "Thank you" came out of Dawayne's mouth. It was the first words he said since he had opened his eyes and seen her dressed up as a French maid. Dawayne was saying thank you, thank you for refilling his drink. Then he started thinking even more, he thankful to have her in his life. He appreciated what she was doing for him, and he said thank you to Serenity again. "This, this is fucking amazing, thank you!" Serenity turned to him with the glass in her hand, "Here."

Dawayne took a sip of the lemonade, and placed it on the floor out of the way. He placed his hands on his head in disbelief, he was staring at pure beauty in front of him.

She walked up to him, moving his legs apart. Sliding between his legs she asked, "What you don't like what you see?" "It's not that at all," Dawayne replied. "This is just too much, this, your fucking amazing." Dawayne placed his hands on the back of Serenity's calves, he brushed his hands along her flesh. Her flesh was warm, and his fingers glided smoothly along her calf. As he moved from her calves, to the back of her knees. He whirled is fingers in rhythm with one another, he started moving towards his favorite attribute. Her thighs, her thighs so long, so slender yet meaty. His fingers slowed their pace, it was as if each of his fingertips had nerve ending that were sending small electric shocks through the muscles in her thighs. She twitch from the energy that was coming from his fingers, a small shock. His fingers eventually found their way to her plump, volleyball booty. As if he had just physically hiked the length of her leg from top to bottom. Dawayne's fingers found the elastic band that was her thong. His fingers hooked around the elastic and he slowly pulled them down, he reached one foot and she lifted her leg up. Placing her hands on his shoulders to hold herself up, then the other leg. Dawayne grabbed the thong and brought it to his nose, he inhaled deeply. Not noticing what he just did, he saw Serenity look at him. He had no explanation, he just told her the truth." I just wanted to smell, then see if you taste, like you smell," Dawayne said at lightning speed, again Serenity looked at him like just spoke a foreign language. She looked at him again and laughed quietly to herself. Serenity then straddled Dawayne, she wiped the sweat off his forehead. Grabbing his neck she went in for a kiss, Dawayne's lips returned the favor. She still had on the high heels, fishnet stockings, and the top. His hands ventured off to her sides, then slowly moving to her breast. He took her neck in his mouth, kissing and licking her with light slow movements.

His hands found her ass again, kneading her cheeks like he was making bread... Dawayne's hands moved along Serenity's vertebrae, stopping at the contraption holding her breast captive. His fingers felt their way to the clips, with a flick here and a flick their bra was hacked. He could feel the warmth that was being held under the bra with the palm of his hand. "It's hot as Africa in here, "Dawayne said. Serenity then got up and walked to turn the heat off and turn the fan on. He was wondering if he was the only one hot as fuck, she rushed back to him and reclaimed her place on his lap. "I fucking love you," Dawayne said with a grin from ear to ear. Serenity looked at him and said I love you too. He finished talking off the top, getting himself wrapped up around her. His arms could almost wrap around her twice, Dawayne repositioned himself on the futon, taking off a layer of clothing. His socks were the first to go, then his shirt was next. "It's really fucking hot in here, I don't want to sweat all over you." "It's only sweat and if it's someone that you know like that, then it's all right." Serenity continued seducing Dawayne, the way she moved reminded him of a snake charmer. He was falling under her spell, her charm, his mind wondered and his imagination went wild. He had never been seduced in a way before, yea he thought he had women that would get in lingerie for him. Yet never did he have a woman put on heels, fishnet stockings and a French maid costume. Dawayne laid back and enjoyed this moment, he would always wonder with his hands. His hands moved slowly along Serenity's long warm body. Serenity kissing him become very dominate in the situation, I'm letting her do her thing he thought to himself. She continued to lure him in, she grabbed at his belt, tugging and pulling she found the clip. Becoming frustrated with the belt, she tugged a lil bit harder. The belt came undone, and slid through a few belt loops on the way off. She attacked his button holding the pants around his waist, then the zipper was next. With enough friction and force to cause sparks, the zipper moved its way down at lightning speed. Serenity pulled at his waist, sliding the pants that he was wearing to the floor. Dawayne was hard, there was no need for a warm up she had done that soon as he saw what she was wearing. Serenity looked at his muscle and put her hands on it, stroking his muscle with a firm grasp and slow. Her movements drug on and he could feel the friction of raw skin to skin contact. To guys they would tap out or bitch out, due to the certain feeling you get with that. Dawayne could feel his muscle rushing blood to the tip, he could feel his muscle stretch to a point that could be pleasurable or quite painful. Lucky for Dawayne he knew that pleasure was on his side tonight, "So I watched a few videos on Bonnie, is that what you really like?" Serenity looked at him waiting for a response, Dawayne looked at her and said," You have been watching my Bonnie?" Serenity laughed, "Is that how you really want it?" Dawayne said yes, and then Serenity looked at him smiled and slowly adjusted herself.

"That's all I needed to know," Serenity moved her lips towards his muscle. In excitement his muscle flexed, as if it knew what sweet treat it was about to receive. He could feel her breath on his tip, he flexed in her grip. She looked at him and then spit on his muscle, spit on her hands. She started rubbing the tip with her two thumbs, slowly sliding her thumbs, then her fingers down the length of his muscle. Once she reached the base she let her fingers climb their way back to the head of his muscle, again she used her thumbs on the tip of his muscle.

This time her warm full lips went around his muscle, she tongued his tip. Flicking it with her tongue, she finished her move with a kiss to the tip. Then she opened her mouth and took his muscle into her wishing well, salivating over his muscle she pulled him out and spit on it again. Serenity took him in her mouth, echoing off the walls sounding like a shop-vac cleaning up a thick wet mess. Dawayne closed his eyes and enjoyed the moment, he wanted to taste her. He wanted to make her feel what he was feeling, given to her what she was giving to him. Serenity had so much suction, so much spit built up. Thinking he was the luckiest man alive, he grinned from ear to ear. Dawayne had to pay her back in the same way, with at least two orgasms. He positioned himself so that he was half way on the futon and floor, and of course her long legs in the air or wrapped around him. He didn't care where he was as long as he was between her long fucking legs. He found himself in a better position than he thought and his tongue went straight into her folds. Moving his tongue slowly between fold to fold, his tongue gliding as if it was a Zamboni after a hockey game. Dawayne moved his fingers towards her sweetness, easing one finger inside it slippery and wet from the nectar she had already extracted. He moved his finger and watched for her body language. Could he tell by the way she moved his head in closer if she liked it? Or her pushing his face from her sweetness, only to find out the only reason this happened. Is that she was going to come, but she didn't want him to know that she was that close to orgasm. Serenity arched he back and moved in closer in his finger, she whirled her hips and bit her lip. Dawayne knew that she was going to come and come like a mother fucker, he felt the balloon swell up. She tried to close her legs, Dawayne used his forearms to hold them in place. "I'm going to make her squirt," he said to himself quietly. He then took his finger and rubbed on her clit with such speed and purpose. "Oh My,God,Rrrrrrraaaaaaaaaaa,Rrrrrrrrrrrrrite there! Oh, god of yes, yes, yes, yessssssssssss. Her legs began to shake, and then he felt it. The warm elixir, he opened his mouth and let the warm liquid hit his tongue. It reminded him of a sour patch kid, it started sour then it got sweet. Dawayne licked his lips, he tasted her come, made her come, made her come more times than she could count. "I want you in me," Serenity growled. Dawayne put one arm behind his back, hoping that he wouldn't have to stop sexually pleasing.

He had some condoms in his pockets, all he had to do was find the pocket. Find the pocket before this session becomes cancelled, or in other words he doesn't get to go deep in Serenity. He had to pull away from Serenity to find the condom, he went from pocket to pocket double checking to see if it was in that pocket. He moved his hands through the pockets, jack pot he thought. He pulled out the golden wrapper and rolled it onto his muscle. He grabbed Serenity by the hips, easing himself in her warm nectar she moaned. He teased her with the tip, he would ease it in just the tip, and then slowly or quickly pull his muscle out." You're a tease, you're a fucking tease," Serenity yelled. That gave Dawayne an even better idea, since she said he was a tease. He was really going you make sure she is teased very well. He pulled his muscle out and slowly glided along the folds of her sweetness. He did this for some time, then he would slowly ease it back inside her walls. Wanting all of it, Dawayne pushed his muscle in real deep and slow, he hit the wall. He went all the way to the natural wall, there was no way that he was going to go any further. His muscle bent, he eased slowly as he pulled himself out. Dawayne found the position that wasn't going to cause either of them any pain, he slowed his rhythm and started to whirl his hips. As his hips moved, Serenity pulled him in closer and dug her fingers into his flesh. Her legs wrapped around him tighter, her fingers became her nails digging into his flesh. As Dawayne felt the nails of Serenity dig into his skin, he only became more aroused. He became even more focused on getting her off one more time, he wasn't done and neither was she. Pulling her legs up in the air, so if he wanted to pull a nigga move he could. He thrusted inside her walls, she moaned and screamed into the pillow. Her body, started to siez and lose all motor skills. "Fuck, fuck, fuck, shit, fuck, god damn, I'm going to come!" "Come for me baby, I'll come with you. I'm almost there wait for me, so we can come together." Serenity tried to control her body but lost the battle. Serenity came and when she came she growled as if the sexual inner goddess had be released and set the fuck free. Dawayne wasn't done yet, he was almost there but she had came before him. He let her get herself in a comfortable position and then he moved her around, so that he could make his nigga move. Serenity lay there on her belly, with her legs wide open and her wet walls pulsating. He pounced on Serenity, and slid inside her. Pulling himself out he looked to make sure he was in the right area.

It was glistening, it was so wet, and sticky from her orgasm. He pulled his muscle to rub on the tip of her clit, then he slid it up to the base of her ass crack. He slowly slid it back down to her clit, and then used his head as a hands to knock on the door of her clit. She jumped the best should could in the position that she was in, and then eased herself back on to his muscle. As she landed back on his muscle he felt his body tense up. He was going to come, when she dropped it on him that was the last nail. He was done for, He held in his orgasm as long as he could, Serenity told him she was going to come again. Finally now was the time that they could come together, "Holy shit, shit, fuck, god damn," Serenity belted in the small room." It echoed off the walls and vibrated through each wall in the building, for all to hear. The best part was that Dawayne didn't give a fuck if anybody heard. All he knew is that he was putting in work and she was about to come again. "Wait for me baby, wait, I'm almost there." Dawayne whispered in her ear, "Come for me baby, come for me," Serenity told him. He felt her walls tighten, his muscle being constricted by her walls made him come. He came with a mighty roar, she came with a loud growl. They came together, they reached another step as a moment, as the king and queen of Elecuphoria.

WEED, SEX, LOVE
&
ADVENTURES

In the following weeks, the love and adventures of Serenity and Dawayne Continued. Dawayne was high off life, he was living a dream. In reality she was in love with him and no one could say anything to change her mind. Serenity started her new job and during orientation she meet Abby, Abby was a dark haired Latina 420 friendly chill chick. Serenity automatically wanted to become friends with her, it didn't hurt that she was attracted to her as well. Abby and Serenity started hanging out during lunch and smoking whenever they got the chance. Hell smoking was the only way to be chill at their job. One night Serenity asked Dawayne if he wanted to go to the Bud Lounge and smoke with Abby and her boyfriend. Dawayne was up for it, it was his first time in a Bud Lounge. Serenity and Dawayne drove to the Bud Lounge, and met Abby and her boyfriend. As they walked into the entrance of the Bud Lounge, the bud host asked for their I.D's and where they wanted to sit. The lounge was nearly empty besides the bud tenders and the few people already enjoying their high. Serenity and Dawayne sat on the same side as Abby and her boyfriend sat across from them. The bud tender introduced himself to them, "Sup people, I'm Gabriel, your bud tender for the evening. Gabe asked them what choice of weapon they wanted to smoke from, showing them the options on the shelf. They all came to a decision and chose one, then they had to choose what flavors they wanted to smoke. They were giving the menu of buds to choose from, Abby and Serenity went through the options, and decided on Sour Patch Kush. In the definition of the SPK, it had a very fruity taste with a hint of sour. The bud tender went to his bar and got the buds, brought them back to the table with the smoking weapon of their choice the bong. Gabriel loaded the bowl for them, asking them if they needed anything else. "Would you like any beverages, or snacks," the bud tender asked. Serenity asked, Sprite? Gabriel gave her the thumbs up, and asked if anybody else wanted anything. Dawayne asked for a sprite as well, and Abby and her boyfriend got bottled water. They sat there and ripped from the bong, passing it to the left starting with Abby and her boyfriend. They smoked and smoked, Gabriel came back and asked if they wanted to try something different. They looked at the menu again, and chose to go with Dragons Blood, when Gabriel came back with the buds Dawayne noticed the bright colors of the buds. Orange hairs, sky blue and lime green buds, and the smell the smell was out of this world amazing.

Serenity to was the first one to spark the buds, she inhaled deeply and blew out the smoke. "That taste fucking amazing," she said. Passing it to Dawayne he inhaled, taking a big hit. Abby's boyfriend and he had been having a who could take the biggest hit challenge. Dawayne's riffs were huge, it helped he had big lungs cause he would take a hit for about twenty-five seconds. They started timing each other to see how long the hits actually were. The closest anyone got to Dawayne was nineteen

Seconds that was Abby's boyfriend. A song came on the speakers in the lounge, and automatically Serenity and Dawayne looked at each other. That look meant they were thinking the same thing, who was the artist and what was the name of the song. Dawayne looked at his phone, Serenity told him to download Shazam to they could find out what song it was. Even though there was an easier way then downloading an app, he continued to search for the app. Downloaded it and soon as he opened the app, the song ended. "Well at least you have it for next time," Serenity said to him. That night they enjoyed good energy and a good time with friends. They asked for the check, split the bill and Serenity and Dawayne headed home. That night they laughed and talked about the good time they had with Abby and her boyfriend. "We'll have to do that again sometime," Dawayne said to Serenity. As fall began to sink into the village, Serenity and Dawayne used the time to explore the little hidden secrets of the village. One night they went to the heart of the village downtown. It was full of life, and energy, the lights from the small business and Bud Shops illuminated the sidewalk. The air was crisp and fresh, with a hint of of the scents from each shop blending together. As they walked arm and hand together, Dawayne had a funny habit of holding Serenity's arm like she was his queen. She told him it was funny, and to just relax and just be in the moment and hold his hand. After a few tries and failing those he got it almost right. They walked into this small book store, they looked around. Serenity went straight to a spot, "It's still here." She said as she held a book with a picture of a a a man and a woman on the cover assuming the position. The Kamu Sutra, Dawayne looked at the book, turned a few pages. As he turned the pages, he would point to the page and position. "Hey we did that one,"pointing at the position The Rising Position. As he points at it he reads it out loud, "The woman raises her legs and rest her calves on his shoulders...after kneeling in front of her and inserting his." Serenity cut him off, as he thumbed through more pages. The Suspended congress, as he reads out again. "As the man stands up the woman jumps into his arms, wrapping her arms around his neck... wrapping her legs around his waist, the man slowly guides..." Serenity cut him off again, as he went through more of the pages he found more and more positions that they have tried. "Well it looks like we've almost done every position in the book, a few rare ones that just look impossible... like ***Reverse Bull Rider***." "That shit looks impossible, Dawayne blurted. The picture had the man on top, like he was doing reverse cowboy yet lying flat and having your head near her feet. They looked at each and laughed, both thinking that a guy on top facing that way was the most complex position in the book. They thanked the person at the desk and headed to the next store. They went into a store that smelt of burning herbs and looked at the décor on the walls. They had old vinyl records, they looked through the records as if they had a record player to play them on. They continued strolling through the village, the night started to whine down. The people walking downtown slowly started leaving the sidewalks, and return to their homes, or the lovers homes, or wherever it was they laid their heads down for the night. Maybe a lonely pillow, an empty apartment. Dawayne looked into Serenity's eyes and said to himself, he was glad he had her in his life. Glad that he took the leap, lived in the moment otherwise he would never be here right now enjoying this moment. He took Serenity by the hand and they walked to the parking garage to the car. They hit the autobahn and headed back to the house. On the way back they hit up a place to get some food, once that was done they headed to the house. Serenity would flirt with Dawayne, and that would most of the time lead to sexual escapades long throughout the night. This night was no different, it started with playful flirting then before you know it he lifted Serenity up onto the counter top. Kissing on her neck and slowly licking and sucking on her earlobes. Serenity moaned, and pulled him in with excitement. He pulled her leggings off, no underwear to worry about. He laid her down onto her back and his mouth went straight to the sweetness, she was already wet and trickling slightly. Slopping it up, he took his tongue and whirled his tongue. She pulled his head in closer, grinding her pussy on his mouth. Sliding her hips, and using his tongue like a cheese grater, she moaned louder. "Yes, right there, right fucking there." Serenity growled out, she was getting ready to come.

He could feel the energy, he could feel that she was going to erupt. "I'm going to come, I'm going to come," Serenity said. Dawayne pulled away from her, he stood in front of her. He stood there naked, somehow he was able to eat her sweets and undress himself at the same time. Nigga shit, she looked at him scooted off the counter top. Put her arms around his shoulders and jumped into his arms, wrapping her legs tightly around his waist. Serenity was so wet, that in the process of jumping into his arms. She slid perfectly on to his muscle, she wasn't able to get the whole thing in but the tip landed at the door mat of her vagina. Dawayne put his arms around her body and moved her in a way that he could fully enjoy her walls. His body slammed up against the wall, with the added force of her weighed onto him. Grabbing her hips he pulled her in slowly, pushing her body away without exiting her walls. The momentum and force increased as Serenity's ass slapped against his thighs with every thrust. Dawayne grabbed onto her ass, and squeezed pulling her in deeper. Moaning and curses to the heavens began to bounce off the walls of the apartment, she could no longer hold her tongue. "Who's dick is that, who's dick is that," Dawayne whispered in her ear. Serenity gasped," That's mine, it's my dick," Dawayne heard that and beast within took over. He carried her to his bedroom, tried to get her off so he could throw her onto the bed. She was holding on, for her dear life, so all he could do is slowly fall onto the bed. He didn't lose his thrust nor did he slide away from her sweetness. Serenity lay on her back, wrapping her thighs around his waist. She pulled him in deeper, her nails slowly digging into his flesh. Dawayne moaned," ohh fuck yea bout time you gotten on my level." Serenity couldn't help herself shit opened her mouth and bit down on his shoulder, she knew what he liked. With that first electric current of sexual energy that is released after being bit hits the brain, Dawayne would go on full bore beat that pussy up mode. That turned Serenity even more sexual and increase her pain tolerance, and then neither would give in to admitting they were defeated.

FML

The season was slowly changing, and so were the colors of the leaves on most the trees. Serenity was looking at her fall bucket list, realizing that fall was almost over and she had not completed her list. Let alone even started it, Dawayne walked by and saw her looking at it, "better get started on that." He said and then laughed and sat on the couch. That weekend they knocked out a good chuck of the list.

*Cafe date by the fire place_*
*Paint a pumpkin_*
*Go on a movie date_*

Things were starting to go really well, almost too well. Dawayne would think, like when you know that things just seem a lil to perfect. Always waiting for that wake up bitch slap the motherfucker we call reality. We are all giving small test in life every day and if we pass or fail them is how the rest of our day will end. When you lay your head down and you can say you had a good day, then you have completed all test today. Dawayne was telling his thought on this, how he see's things. Serenity chucked and continued to listen. Fall past and the beginning of winter hit, early November right around Serenity's birthday. One morning Dawayne woke up, he knew what day it was so he had to make it a special one. He went to the local grocer and got a card, made a key, and some skittles to finish it off. He put together all the supplies together in the kitchen once he got home. Even just the thought of actually doing something so sweet made him laugh. When she woke up she saw the Lili's and skittles, opened the card and read the words. You have the key to my heart, now you have the key to my place. She looked at him kissed him, hugged him and didn't want to let go. " A good way to start your day, Happy Birthday." That afternoon he surprised her by taking her out to lunch, and he had a surprise up his sleeve for later on that evening. Once he got home he looked up the info he was looking for. So that evening they made a night of her birthday, and it was a morning to never forget. Dawayne waited until 1:20am then they left his place, and headed for the autobahn. As he was driving she was wondering where they would be going this early in the morning. Dawayne kept his mouth closed but the smile on his face, shown that whatever it was it was going to be good. He started driving down n the red light district, a sign illuminated from the corner of Serenity's eye as he turned right. Euphoria's Gentlemen Club, sign was shining bright red. Serenity all of a sudden got excited, Dawayne pulled into the parking lot and parked. As both of them got out the car, there was a man puking on the side of a truck and his friends continued on without him. Dawayne handed Serenity $20 in singles and said, "Happy fucking birthday!" They walked to the main entrance, soon as they walked in both of their eyes focused on a light skinned beauty. "I want a lap dance from her," Serenity said Dawayne was already thinking that. He paid the cover charge and they found a nice spot at the end of the stage. Serenity was excited she could barely keep her composure. As the time passed by they were waiting for the light skinned beauty to come up on stage. As each dancer did their routine, the light skinned beauty was nowhere to be found. "Coming up on stage next Juicy Jennifer," the dj said into the mic. That's when she came out a white girl with a fat ass, Serenity could see what Dawayne was talking about. "What you think about her," Dawayne said. Serenity said with a low tone," I'm not sure I don't know I would have to get a better look." "Then throw down some singles," he said as he took a fold out and built a pyramid with singles to get the dancers attention. She came over and bounced her ass in his face, and rubbed her titties in his face. Serenity was then able to see what he was talking about and laid down singles of her own. The dancer looked at Serenity and began to ask her a few question, "You like girls, the dancer asked?" Serenity smiled and answered back, "Yes." At first Serenity was hesitant, she wasn't sure what to do. It was the first time she had ever been in a strip club, but it was something they could both enjoy and have a good time doing together. The Juicy Jennifer did a lil routine for Serenity and you could tell it got her all hot and wet. After that she wanted more, but they were both still waiting for the light skinned beauty. As Dawayne and Serenity looked around they saw two light skinned girls, they were persuading a few gentlemen to purchase lap-dances." I want a dance with one of those two girls, I'll take the one with the gold outfit on, Serenity said with a big ass grin on her face. They had fun that morning, and as the the club slowly started to whined down, the dancers started to call it a day and slip into their everyday clothes. Before they knew it the dj was calling last call, and they had still not received a lap-dance from either light skinned beauty. During all the other dancers, that performed on stage the bad bitches decided to spend their time giving lap-dances to other people besides them.

Dawayne and Serenity were a lil sad, but they still had a great time, and it was a good mother fucking birthday ending it ending in the bed with his Queen. It was only a few days after and more task were completed on her fall bucket list. Dawayne had taken Serenity out to the local Starbucks. Starbucks date was not very far from the bottom, but Serenity had skipped around on her list. They sat near the fire place and listened too other peoples conversations. That was a lil thing they would do, and when they were alone they would talk about the stories that they heard. Dawayne started telling a story, they laughed and joked about it. The both of the over exaggerating the parts of the stories. Dawayne started telling Serenity about a bonfire out of the village, one of his friends was having that Saturday. He said that there was going to be a band playing at the party, and it was different kind of pot luck party, the 420 friendly kind of pot luck. The week past slowly as it would as you're anticipating something fun at the end of your busy week. That Saturday Dawayne got off work later than normal. He locked the kitchen up and headed to his car, thinking what to bring to the party. Since he got off work thirty minutes later than normal. On his way home, the idea popped into his head. He would stop by the pizzeria that was a few blocks from his house. He would stop there order pizzas, get back to the apartment take a shower, Then Serenity and him would pick the pizzas and head up to the bonfire. When he got in town plan rolled out just as he had thought, they took a shower together and got dressed. Both of them in black, they headed out the door and hit up the pizzeria. Dawayne got out the car and went inside, coming out with twelve pizzas in his hands. Six pepperoni and six cheese, for the vegetarians a lot of people in the village were vegetarians. It was more of a hippy town, people were way more laid back and comfortable with everyday stresses of life. He opened the back door, and proceeded to put the pizzas in the back seat. Serenity looked at him and said "Put the pizzas on my lap, they'll keep me warm. Dawayne laughed and shut the back door handing them to her a few pizzas at a time. Shut the door gentle and ran to the the driver seat. "It's fucking cold a fuck out there. There better be a big ass mother fucking bonfire there to keep people warm. They drove on the autobahn, then head up. As they drove closer to the hippy house the amber glow brightened, "There's your big ass mother fucking bonfire." She said with sarcasm, the parking area was the size of a small parking lot.

There weren't many spots to park, so he parked up on the snow. He opened his door and stepped into snow, filling his shoe with snow. He stepped to where the snow had been packed down, walking to open the door and take a few pizzas out of her hands so she could get out with seeing. The pizzas were stacked up so he she could barely see in front of her. He took half the stack, and lightened her load. They both walked carefully threw through the snow. Before they made it to the front door, somebody opened the door. As the door opened smoke came swooping outside and drifted straight towards the bone-fire. The smell of the village's finest Kush, was fumigating most of the area around the fire. They walked in and a white girl with dreadlocks, showed them to the kitchen. Placing the pizzas on the counter top, Dawayne grabbed a slice and walked out to the living room. Introducing Serenity to his friends and co-workers, and those he didn't know introduced themselves to them. They went outside to check out the bonfire it was one big mother fucking bonfire. As the came closer to the fire, they heard music. It was coming from the garage around the corner it was a fucking band. The walked to the bonfire, people were laying in the snow and just enjoying the heat radiating from all the pallets they found. Serenity grabbed Dawayne's hands and eased them around her waist. He squeezed just enough to get a reaction, she turned her head up to his. He kissed her forehead, whispering I love you in her ear. They stood there by the fire for a while, as the marijuana smoke circulated around the fire the smell of fire a wood turned Serenity on, she pushed her ass back slowly teasing him. He pulled her in while slowly moving his arms to wrap around her chest. The sexual energy was starting to rebuild, they needed to leave and go home. They left the fire and headed to the house, making sure to say thank you and good bye to people. Walking through the house to say good bye they saw all the pizza was gone, they both chuckled and continued through the house. Most the people had cleared out there was a few people in the living room and few people passed out on the floor. Bypassing the snow this time Dawayne was able to get in the car. Serenity was shivering, Dawayne turned the key and the heater turned on. They got to the house, as they walked in Serenity said," I fucking love the smell of bonfire or campfires on clothes!" They didn't make it very far, Dawayne started taking her clothes off. Serenity stepped out of her pants as he stepped on them to allow her to ease out of them.

He sucked on the cove of her neck, the smell of fire was strong and sensual. He pulled his belt off and unbuttoned his jeans, pulling his pants down with one hand. High stepping out of his jeans, pulling back on Serenity's neck and biting down gently. He turned her around and picked her up, laying her down on the counter top. He pushed whatever was on the counter out of the way, and laid Serenity down slowly. He eased inside her folds, she was wet, and he slid in and pulled her body closer to him. He pulled out and got on his knees, he started licking her sweetness. She moaned and tried to push him away, he pulled her thighs in so he could wrap his arms around her thighs and hold them. He continued to lick her pussy, she moaned and bit her lip, cussing and rambling words that she just created. He stood up and flicked her clit with the head of his muscle, like he was knocking on a door. She pushed herself into him, trying to be slick and get that dick inside her. He knew what she was trying to do, he was in control. She would get the dick when he was ready to give it to her and she begged for it. He kept teasing her for a while slowly entering the walls of her pussy, then he would stop just before all the head would disappear. This shit drove her crazy, she was doing her best trying to pull him in closer. Only thing is Dawayne was in control, she started to say something. That's when he pulled her in and started rapidly fucking the shit out of her, whatever she was going to say she forgot. He slowed his pace let her come to, he went back to slowly easing inside of her with just the tip. She started to say something, he pulled her by the ass and lifted her up. Still inside her, he held her in the air. Thrusting his muscle deep inside her walls, he pounded that pussy giving Serenity the satisfaction of finally getting the dick. He carried her to the room, meanwhile never losing a stroke along the way. He slowed his pace, and carefully walk down the hallway without bumping into anything. All while still sliding in and out of her so wet and oh so tight pussy. He tossed her on the bed as gentle as one could, and reached in the closet for a condom. He found one hidden behind his clothes, he ripped the package open with his teeth and slid it on his dick. Serenity called his name, he whispered in hers, he pulled himself deep against her wall. Bending his muscle, she pulled away a bit. He gave it to her deep, that's how she liked it, even though after it would be a bit. He pulled deeper, flipping her to her side and chose a different position. To help with her comfort and he could have more control on his depth.

He didn't want to create any more damage to her walls if he could help himself. The sun began to rise, and they had just ended their session. Exhausted and covered with the scent of fire, smoke and sex. Dawayne rolled over kissed Serenity on the neck, kissed each nipple, kissed her right hip. Whispered in her ear he loved her, and headed to the shower to get ready for work. He turned on the music, turned the shower on and shut the door. The smell of fire, smoke and sex found its way down the drain, while Dawayne's body saturated the scent from his Dove body wash. A few days went by, as more things off Serenity's fall bucket list were completed. There was one that she was unsure of, title SHROOM NIGHT. Well that day Serenity got her wish to come true, her friend Abby had text Serenity letting her know she could get some mushrooms. Dawayne received a text from Serenity.

Hey
Do
You
Wanna
Trip
On
Shrooms
Tonight
Abby can get us some
So what you say

Dawayne looked at the text, and replied back with the letters in text LITM. Live in the Moment, Dawayne thought to himself. Thinking like what's the worst that can happen have a bad trip, and never do shrooms again. He was just getting off work so he had to drive on the autobahn in 5o'clock rush. He drove home with some many ideas of how the night would go. He thought maybe Serenity, Abby, and himself would have a crazy threesome. It would be a night to remember, or it could be what was not expected. Nothing could happen and they would be waiting for the trip to start, when it already has but weak shrooms. Or it could be his dream come true trip, they watch a scary movie and it actually freaks him the fuck out. That good scare that you got when you were a kid and something scared you and you couldn't sleep without a night light on. That trip would be the best for Dawayne, he wanted to trip to the point of no return of adrenaline to the brain and heart.

He pulled up in his parking spot looking up on the balcony, Serenity and Abby were outside smoking. He walked up the stairs and stopped to talk to them. Abby was excited for Dawayne and Serenity to take the shrooms. They walked into the kitchen, Abby pulled the baggie out of her coat. She divided the caps between the two of them, some stems and some caps. Trying to give equal amounts by the different sizes of caps and stems. There was a few small caps Abby put those to the side for herself. "Alright mother fucker's ready to trip fucking balls, well soon it takes a while for them to hit. Once they do watch out mother fuckers, cause they going to take you on a trip." Serenity looked at Dawayne, he looked at her and popped what was in his hand into his mouth. He chewed and chewed until there were nothing left, opening his mouth and sticking out his tongue. To show Serenity that there was nothing left in his mouth. Serenity popped a stem into her mouth and did her best to chew it up. Abby passed her what was left of her orange juice. Dawayne went to the TV, and went to pick out a movie. Tenacious D and the pick of Destiny, was his choice. He also had the Wiz, both versions. The one with Michael Jackson, and the newer version with Ne-Yo. He hit the play button, and the movie began. Dawayne laughed as he saw the facial reactions Abby and Serenity, were giving during the start of the movie. "This movie was made for people who smoke weed and trip acid and shrooms. He looked at his phone and remembered he had to be somewhere in ten minutes. He told the ladies that he would be right back, "Are you ok to drive." Serenity asked, Dawayne gave her the thumbs up," I'll be fine they still have like thirty more minutes till they hit. I will be back way before they hit, kk." He said I love you and headed out the door. He walked slowly down the stairs, the sun was so bright. Brighter than normal he thought, He got in his car, he turned the key. He turned the music up and drove, looking at the stoplight still on red he looked into his rear view mirror. The road behind him was rolling towards him like a huge wave of asphalt. It was moving slowly towards him, and the light was still fucking red. His anxiety started to overtake him, he continued looking into his rear view mirror. The wave of asphalt was almost to him, he thought if he needed to he would run the red light. The light turned green and he speed up and drove over the canal. He didn't look back until he was in his parking spot again, and the front of his apartment was in clear view.

He opened his eyes Dawayne was sweating, he looked in his hands the keys were still in his hands. He put the keys into the ignition, back pedaling trying to think if he even left the parking lot. He didn't have anything new in his car, no grocery bags, no nothing. He thought maybe he didn't even leave the parking lot, he looked at the clock on his dashboard. It flashed but dim 6" o clock. Thirty minutes passed the time he left the apartment. He headed up the stairs looked around, seeing if anybody could see him. He opened the door it was dark in his apartment, but it was easier on the eyes than that bright ass sun. He walked in, "I think I'm tripping pretty good now!" Serenity looked at Dawayne, she looked into his eyes," Damn your pupils are HUGE as FUCK." "So are yours," Dawayne said as Abby laughed at the both of them. They sat and watched the movie," What the fuck is going on in this movie," Serenity yelled. As Jack Black turned into a baby big foot. Abby looked at her phone, she got up and said her good byes." Got to go?" Serenity asked. Telling them "See all you later bitches," and closing the door behind her. Dawayne went to the computer and picked a different movie, the Wiz. He choose the play with Ne-Yo, they had both been anticipating watching it. To see how close they are to the original, within moments Serenity was blowing hot air. "This isn't even how it started," Dawayne tried to take the attention of the horrible reenactment of the Wiz. He began to kiss her neck, and move his hands up and down her thighs. Squeezing ever so slightly, when he would round near the bottom of her ass. He put his lips on her thighs, sliding his tongue on any exposed flesh below the belt. He grabbed her button and undid it, slowly pulling her shorts off. He looked at Serenity and started to slide his pants off, he pulled on himself and slid himself right inside. She said quite quietly that T.O.M might be coming soon. He continued thinking that they've done it before it couldn't be that bad, what a lil blood is going to hurt. He slid inside her walls and the sensation was more, the feeling was something he couldn't find the words for. Serenity felt so good, she was so wet, and she was feeling it to. She pulled herself closer to him, and then the shrooms kicked in. Dawayne could hear the sounds of everything, like every sound in the room clear as day. He could hear he natural nectar escaping from her inner walls, flooding out as if she had built a dam and it was destroyed by the muscle. He looked down and saw blood, there was so much blood he stopped his stroke.

Switched the way his hands were on her legs, he could see hand prints of blood on her thighs. He pulled out, Serenity looked at him like WTF, and he looked back down. There was no blood, there was just a wet as pussy, wetter than normal. He grabbed himself and slowly slid his way back to the pussy, along the way he brushed along her ass. "Hey no, Serenity said to him. Dawayne listened to her he was not attempting to go anal, just got lost on the trip. He was able to slide into the right spot, the spot that felt so fucking good, she was so goddamn tight, and wet. He looked back down again, blood was everywhere? Blood was on the couch, blood was all over both of them. Once again the shrooms had a major effect on his mind, he closed his eyes and opened them. The blood was gone, it was just them in the room with the background noise of the Wiz on. Dawayne was trippin, he looked at Serenity and wanted to be inside her again. He moved on the couch and switched his position, with her legs around him he just wanted this trip to end so he could enjoy her. This was a lil too much for him the shrooms, sex, he guided himself slowly from her ass to her sweetness. He did this a few times, and then he heard her scream. He was in her ass, soon as he was in there he knew it was the wrong spot. He could feel how contracted it was and the pressure, that was unfamiliar territory. Dawayne jumped off Serenity, and ran to the shower. While he turned the shower on he turned up the music, he couldn't believe what had just happened. He didn't even know where he was until it was too late. She had told him No to anal, and he had just attempted for a second time. Dawayne saw the look that Serenity had in her eyes, there was nothing their anymore. Everything that he knew about serenity changed that moment, he saw pain, hurt, and anger in her eyes, and love was gone. He saw that look and thought of what a horrible person he was, he didn't want to live. He wanted to die, dying was better than having to look at her again. Dying would make things even, he had took her trust, took whatever good spirits she had, and ripped them away. With one stupid act, and these fucking shrooms. He jumped in the shower, not knowing that Serenity was in the living room trying to comprehend all of the emotions erupting inside of her. While Serenity was in the living room containing herself, Dawayne was in the shower crying. He broke the trust with the one person that he had tried to never hurt, she was his one and only. The last thing he ever wanted to do was lose her trust, lose her love, and lose everything they have built together.

So many things were going through his mind at the moment, it was too much to take. His anxiety kicked in, his breath came out choppy. It seemed as if all the weight in the world was now on his chest, he tried to breathe slowly, he tried to close his eyes and take deep breaths. He turned up the temp on the water, he needed some scalding water. He needed to wash the whole situation away, like that was going to happen. He closed his eyes, opening them once again he saw blood. The blood flowing down the drain of the tub, he had blood running all down his legs. He looked at his hands the blood vanished, then came back. The blood was coming in and out the way clouds on a sunny day cover the sun. Was this trip ever going to end, did he really try to do anal on her. The music continued to play, and he tried his best to wash the cold hard facts down the drain. He took the longest shower ever, he kept turning up the heat until the water that pelted off of him was luke warm. Dawayne heard foot steps to the bedroom, his heart began to race. He heard the door open and he opened the shower curtain, there Serenity stood. With a gun in her hand pointed straight at him, she squeezed the trigger, and he closed his eyes. He could feel the blood flow rushed to his head, he grabbed the wall. He almost slipped getting out of the shower, he reached for his towel took two steps and fell to his bed. When he came to, he was drained his body temp started to fall. Naked on the bed laying on his towel he rolled over to his side, looking for a bullet wound. That's when he realized it was all part of a horrible trip, he tried to think how long he was out. He realized what had just happened moments before, he tip toed to the kitchen the movie was still playing and Serenity was in the bathroom. The energy in the room was off, something was wrong, then he remembered what he tried to do. He closed his eyes and vowed never to trip on shrooms ever again. Dawayne knew once that door opened what they were was no longer, what they had could not be rebuilt. The trust she had in him was gone, he was a beast. He failed her, he failed himself, and he failed everything that he was trying to do with this moment he shared with Serenity. After that day THEY were never the same.

SECOND
CHANCES
&
FORGIVENESS

As the days passed and the mental rip slowly healed, Dawayne tried to find himself. He was in a low place, he never felt so bad. He did his best to make things right between them but, as all know trust is the biggest piece in any relationship. He knew the chances of ever having her trust again would be slim if even that. Dawayne learned from this mistake, he took the time to really comprehend what he did wrong, and that he still had control of his actions. The shrooms could not be used an excuse and wouldn't be, he maned up and confessed to himself what he did wrong. He then said he'd never make a stupid mistake like that again. It took a while for Serenity to forgive Dawayne, he waited patiently for weeks before she could even look him in the eye. By this time the holidays were coming to a near and Serenity was going to spend the holiday with family. During this time they decided to knock off as many things as they could off her bucket list. Serenity knew that it was from her fall bucket list, but they could still be done. They headed to the local book store with pieces of paper and pens. They wrote little notes to the lucky person that just happen to open the book, on the page the note was neatly placed. They would write fake endings to the book they were hidden it, to in a messed up fucked up kind of way. Be a spoiler alert to the end of the book, but they had no idea on how the books actually ended. They each had six pieces of paper, and went around in the book store, thinking of clever ending to books they just read as a glance, saw the same of a character and think. They walked around for about fifteen minutes, just going around the book store. They bumped into each other, Dawayne showed the ending to Serenity.

John finds out that
Stacy was the one that
That killed everybody

Serenity looked at it and laughed loud, peopled turned to see if they has missed out on seeing something worth a laugh like that. Serenity showed Dawayne what her note had read.

Susan wakes up from a dream
What she thought was
A dream
It all happened on video
Live
Her life was ruined
She took her own life
LIVE ON AIR
This is the REASON the Trutube DIED

'Damn," Dawayne looked at it, that's some deep as shit. It almost sounds way too real. What if that was they note that was the actual ending?" They both looked at each other and laughed again, going their ways until they ran out of note paper. They meet up at the entrance, and headed out the door. Not forgetting to say thank you to the person behind the counter. They headed down town to see if the Kama Sutra book was still there, that they had seen in the fall. They got out the car and walked hand in hand, Dawayne took Serenity's arm into his as if it was more gentleman like. Serenity laughed at him, "why you do that?" she asked. Dawayne had an answer but it wasn't what he wanted to tell her at the moment. He came up with some shit at the top of his head to satisfy Serenity's curiosity. The looked for cute hidden bookstore hidden downtown, it was on the other side of the road. They both looked at each other and laughed, they waited for the traffic to ease so they could cross the road to the book store. They crossed the road, Dawayne opened the door for Serenity and followed behind. She headed straight for where it was last time, she lifted it off the shelf. Flipping the book over, to see if anyway it was a different book.

"That Kama Sutra books, still fucking there. Damn" Dawayne tried to say quietly as the lady at the counter turned and asked if they needed any help. They both shook their heads, saying at the same time no thanks. Serenity put the book back where it was secretly hidden, with books of not the same genre. They walked out the book store and walked around some more, just breathing and enjoying the fresh winter air. It had not yet snowed in the valley yet, so it was nice winter weather perfect. The next night, Dawayne took her out to see a scary movie. They hit up the candy store before they got to the movie theater. They got their favorite candies and paid and headed onto the autobahn, the quickest route to the movie theater. They arrived with a few minutes to spare before the movie started, Dawayne paid for their tickets and they paid for a shared drink. Walking to the entrance of the theater, the ticket holders asked for their tickets. Dawayne handed them to the young man, and he handed them the stub. "Enjoy your movie, you two are going to be in theater 7." "That's will be to your right and up the ramp." They walked down the hall and up the ramp, entering theater 7. Dawayne and Serenity looked around they were the only a handful of people in the theater. Looking for a good spot, Serenity pointed to one Dawayne nodded and they headed up the stairs towards the high deck. He let Serenity go in first, there was nobody within rows of them. She found the seat she was looking for, "Here," she said quietly and she sat down getting situated. Dawayne sat down deciding whether to take off his jacket or leave it on. Finally deciding to just leave the jacket on, it always did seem like it gets chilly in the theaters once the movie starts and the lights begin to dim. It was a good choice during the movie, because it got chilly quick. Dawayne gave Serenity the look, like this movie is not as good as the previews made it out to be. They sat through the rest of the movie, then roasted it afterwards as the left the theater. The night after that they went to race go-carts. It was all about enjoying a good time and good vibes, Serenity was getting ready to leave in the next few day. So they had to soak up all the moments up as they could. They raced Serenity had a blast, Dawayne followed behind her for a while until she got the hang of it.

Then it was time to race and to his amazement she ended up whipping his ass, it was close but she still beat him on the last lap. The last few days went by so fast and the next thing Dawayne knew it. He was waking up early to take her to the rail station. He hit the autobahn, and hit the exit where the bus station was located. Serenity told him that she was making a big mistake going down for the holidays. She felt like this decision she made was wrong and that leaving, well the universe had no help in her decision. She didn't want to leave him but she wanted to see her family it had been a while since she had seen them. The bus arrived behind schedule and the travelers got off the bus and collected their belongings. Dawayne gave Serenity a big hug, wishing she would stay with him. It being in the back of his mind wanting to say, but he just held back. He wanted her to have a good time with her family, he wasn't doing anything big for the holiday. Work and spend the rest of the day watching movies on Netflix. They said their goodbyes, she held him tight he whispered something sweet and positive in her ear and he released his grip on her. Every time she left him she cried, he always tried to wrap his head around it. Always wondering why it always felt like leaving was a bad thing, then why did she leave him every time. He thought one day he would learn, he would not let the feelings he had in control. Not to FEAR of the uncertain, because you never know. Serenity hugged him one last time with tears in her eyes like she was going to be leaving forever, tears running down her cheeks. She tried to wipe the tears before it made her eye liner run but it was too late. During the holiday they had each bought each other something of special moments. Dawayne went to the little book store downtown village and bought that Kama Sutra book. He was so happy that it was still there he flipped through the book, checking off with his finger all the positions he had already done with serenity. He had a few more things for her the Rihanna Limited Edition gift set of smell goods. Before the big holiday hit he wrapped Serenity's gifts.

Hope that there would be a small chance that she was just fucking with him, and she was going to surprise him for the holiday. As life always seemed to be so blunt he was hit with the reality that she wasn't going to be able to be with him during the holiday. So Dawayne was left to face the holiday alone, he stayed busy and before he knew it Serenity was telling him she was going to Mihai city.

Dawayne had a gut feeling that she was going to hook up with her girlfriend while she was there, that would only be the reason why she would go there. Then like during holiday, he felt her steer away from him. She told him that she was with her and was going to stay with her until the New Year. He tried to not think about it, Serenity with her but it took over his dreams. He was unable to sleep for a number of nights. He started fighting the battle in his dreams. Dawayne just had to not waste his energy and time on thinking of what could happen, and what would happen. If Serenity ended up hooking up with her girlfriend then so be it. So that came to him with clarity, that no matter how much he loved someone he could not have any control over events not in his hands or the universe. That was life, you get to be the driver of your life but sometimes it has glitches and you get stuck in auto- pilot. He slept well the rest of the break, until one night he had such a vivid and realistic dream that woke him from a deep sleep. He tried not to think about it, he went into his bathroom lit a bowl and listened to some music to sooth his mind. He laid back down and feel asleep with no problems. Serenity rarely text him or called him while she was with her, at this point and time Dawayne already knew. He might not have had evidence but he had seen this behavior before and he knew he was no longer the person in Serenity's life that she loved with everything in her being. It was almost time for her to come back, she slowly started talking to

Dawayne again, but it wasn't the same as it was before. Something had changed, the energy that was coming from her was drained, the good vibes slowly started to wither away as well. Serenity told him when she was coming back and he prepared himself for the worst and for honesty. He found himself waiting for her early in the morning at the train station, even though in the back of his mind he didn't want to be there. He felt as if Serenity had already made her decision and that wasn't with him. So he thought while he was waiting for the bus, to just be open minded about it all, no reason to judge, or have his guard put up. He knew the situation he put himself in by falling in love with a young woman that had a girlfriend. That's why live in the moment was such a good definition of them, they were a fucked up relationship. Yet it worked for them and that's all that mattered to them. Serenity got off the train, the vibe felt the same as if was before. There was something that she was holding back, but he knew in time that she would open up and tell him what was on her mind.

Things went to the way they were before. A few days later Serenity to so excited, "Your Package is here." She said all excited and unable to control herself. Dawayne went into his bedroom and pulled out the one package he wrapped, he looked at the Kama Sutra book. For some reason he told himself that the book could wait, for another time. He brought the package out of the bedroom and put it on the counter top next to Serenity's package. He say her eyes get all big, but she still insisted on him opening his first. So Dawayne opened up the package it was a blanket with pictures of the good memories they shared under the flash. He was excited and oddly saddened at the same time he couldn't figure out why he was feeling sad, he should be happy sadness shouldn't even be close to this place he thought. He pushed Serenity's gift in between her hands, Serenity she slowly opened her package she saw the colors. Her pupils widened, then she saw the letter spelling Rihanna Limited Edition. "The box is so fucking beautiful, I don't even want to open up the box." Serenity opened the box and saw the three special edition beautifully crafted bottles. She took of the lid to each one and slowly inhaled, "I bet this is what her vagina smells like!" The both of them started busting up, Dawayne nodded his head in compliance. They both took their gifts and put them back in their boxes. They said there thank you, and left their gifts on the counter top, almost as if they were to never be actually used. It wasn't long before she was telling him that he needed to shave. That was the code word for, shave and you'll get to eat this pussy and then you be able to fuck me till I need my inhaler. He shaved that morning and and in minutes he was on his belly, and in between Serenity's thighs. He would let his tongue just slowly wonder over every inch, her sweet nectar slowly started to seep out. Dawayne got his tongue and slowly licked the sweet juice. Serenity gasped, as if it had been long time since she had been pleased like that. He grabbed for his muscle, as if it was something she had been craving. Serenity wasn't sure if she liked the way it vibed anymore, she knew she like the way Dawayne felt inside of her. Dawayne spent a few hours to get reacquainted with that sweet pussy he longed for it, he couldn't wait for the next time he got the chance to enjoy her, devour her. There was something more passionate about it this time, like Serenity was giving herself to him all over again. She started almost crying, he could see the water in her eyes filling her lids. "Do you want me to stop," Dawayne asked "No," Serenity said as she pulled him deeper.

They made love for a duration of the evening and into the beginning of the morning. It was intense, sensual, primal, mental and emotional. By the time they were done, they were both drained and just laid there on their backs afterwards. Breathing hard and sweat glistening off their skin, Serenity rolled onto her side and looked into Dawayne's eyes. Her eyes began to water, Dawayne was starting to get a real strong unusual vibe from Serenity. She looked at him, making sure not to look him straight in the eyes. She said with tears running down her cheek, "I'm engaged!" Dawayne had to wrap his head around what she had just told him, he rolled on to his side. He had a look of heart break in his eyes, his heart had been filleted like a fish. All he could do was look at her and give her comfort as if he didn't feel anything. Even though his heart had just been tenderized by the hammer of reality, he found something to keep him from falling apart. That would be the last thing he would ever let any woman see in him, his emotions where locked deep. Before he took his arms around her to consult her, he didn't want to make the same mistakes he made in the past. He asked her if she was alright, "Serenity I know when something is up. You know I know this and something is wrong, you can tell me whatever it is." Serenity told him how she had some strong energy telling her that she should have stayed with him during Holiday. "I'm so stupid," Serenity said. "I always find a way to fuck things up, when I have a somebody that loves me for me and all that is me. I fucking find a way to fuck it up!" She told him that while she was with her, she had also lost her job. Serenity was to be back before the New Year, and she decided to spend her time with her. She was so mad at herself for losing her job, they had worked with her to the perfect shifts with great hours. There was so much energy that was being drained Serenity, whenever she was with her. Serenity was telling him that everybody tells her that, her FIANCE sucks the life from her. How your partner is supposed to be positive, and how negative she actually made it. Dawayne took both his hands and placed them on her cheeks, and he looked into her eyes and said. "Serenity for fucking human, we don't make mistakes we make choices. That was a choice you made, and it is what it is." Serenity looked at Dawayne tears still running down her cheeks, "why can't she have what you have, like be like you? Why couldn't you've been born a girl?" Dawayne didn't snap back, although he wanted too. He thought that he loved Serenity for Serenity.

He would never even think of asking her to change, lesbian, or bi-sexual, pans he didn't care. Dawayne loved her and what she was, what made her, all the lil things that made him laugh.

He smiled and said," If I was born a chick, we would of never CONNECTED. I don't even know where I would be right now. I wish we could switch hearts, I wish we could switch places." He smiled gave her a kiss on the for head, told her he loved her for who she was. He rolled up and walked to the bathroom. Dawayne hooked up his phone to the speaker and turned up the music, turned the water on. He looked for something to smoke but there was nothing in site, he hit the shower knob. He picked a song, Falling Up by So Mo. He turned the song up, in a way hoping that Serenity would hear the song. Maybe hear the lyrics and maybe in some crazy way know how he was feeling by the song he decided to play. Pulling the shower curtain back, he stepped into the shower. Pulling the shower curtain closed he moved the shower head so that it would hit him right in the face. Putting his head down the hot water trickled down his neck, then down his back. The sting of the heat slowly beading down his spine, caused him to feel something. Dawayne arched his back. As if just the action alone would ease the pain, he wondered if he stayed under the hot scolding water. He wondered if it could also melt the pain away that was in his heart. The ore would slowly harden around his heart if he was strong enough, and it would create an armor. Dawayne still standing in the shower was having a deep connection with reality. He realized that each action does have an equal and opposite reaction, he had broken a heart or two. Sooner or later it catches up to you Karma. Only know did he know what it felt like, it only took him 100 years to finally have his heart broken. Clarity was in his mind and in his heart, he could handle this two ways. He could be angry about the situation, he can hold a grudge. The other choice was the harder of the two, he had to open up to the concept of letting it go. He turned the water as far as the knob would go, the heat came back slowly. He had told Serenity that she was only human, we all make choices. Now he had to make the choice, thinking that what happened. Happened and the only thing to do was move forward, a familiar sound in the bathroom caught his attention. The next thing he knew Serenity was behind him in the shower, she was shivering like she had been outside in the winter weather. He switched his position and let Serenity pass him, as she did she was grazed by the slowly hardening of his man below.

She stood in front of the shower, Dawayne stood back and let her have more room. But enough room he was still close to her, he had the idea of bending her over and giving her the Nigga Dick. He thought about it, he wanted to give it to her so fucking bad. Then something struck him, and the idea went away. He wrapped his arms around Serenity, gave her a hug and kissed her on the neck. Whispering I love you in her ear, he turned and left the shower. Dawayne believed what THEY had was over and a new relationship was built that morning. He would no longer see Serenity as his one and only, sadly. Yet she was his one and only lesbian love. So he laughed about it and looked at the tattoo on his wrist, reading Live in the Moment. He thought he had been living in the moment, he had let loose, let his guard down and just decided to LIVE. Ever since Serenity asked him if the letters on the note were I Can Make Your Dreams Come True, he had lived in the moment. Every moment besides that shrooms night and last night, life has treated him pretty fucking good. So this was the start of another moment, Dawayne finished drying himself off and put on some clothes and headed for the kitchen. He got his keys walked back into the bedroom and told Serenity that he was going to be right back that he just had to get out. "Can I come with you?" Serenity asked, Dawayne told her he just needed some time to himself. He opened the front door, closing it behind him. He went to his car, turned the key put it in reverse and pulled out of his parking spot. He drove about two miles and then he cursed at whoever was listening. "I give my all, I pour my heart out, and I open up emotionally!" This is what I fucking get, this is what I get for cheating on my ex. Mother FUCKING KARMA, and she is a BAD bitch." Dawayne was looking around seeing if anybody saw him talking to himself, he chuckled thinking how crazy he would have looked if someone did see him. He turned into a vacant parking lot, took a minute to wrap everything. Everything that just happened at the apartment, he took his phone into his hands and went through his music. Stopping at a song from one of his play-list, and Falling on My Face by BJ the Chicago Kid echoed and vibrated in his car. The song ended and he turned onto the on ramp to get him back home, his parking spot was still vacant, the morning frost slowly turned into dew drops. He walked up the stairs with a different feeling, a different understanding, and was ready for whatever life threw at him this time.

THE
BOX
OF MEMORIES

It was only a few days after that Dawayne came to Serenity with an idea. He told her that they should put everything they have gave to each other should go in a box. They needed to collect all the letters, every note, any gift. Even the most recent gifts they had given each other, yet never really used or opened after that night. They went into the rooms and collected all the things, Dawayne found a box that could fit most of it he hoped. Dawayne even grabbed the matching hoodie's that Serenity had bought them. He could tell by the look in Serenity's eyes this was painful. Jamming all the memories and gifts they ever bought each other in a box, and this box wouldn't be opened any time in the near future. Dawayne put a couple full three ring binders, full of letters going as far back as the first note Serenity ever gave him. Inside Dawayne was at peace, he told Serenity his idea on how long these items shall remain in the box. "The box can never be opened unless, both people are present. I will carry the box of memories with me where ever I go. That's a good name box of memories, the BOM!" They laughed and tried to lighten the energy, it was hard for both of them, Serenity looked at it they may NEVER open the box. Dawayne looked at Serenity, "Is that everything you have, I put everything you ever gave me in there. I have a lil feeling that you're holding out on me." Serenity pulled out an envelope full of letters that were hand written top her by him. "Put those in the BOM, nothing can be left behind. Everything has to be sealed up." Serenity put the envelope in box inside the box, while she was doing this she rearranged the way the items were. "Is that necessary, you just want to touch all of that before it gets locked up." Dawayne laughed, he grabbed the Rihanna box, and it was the last thing to go. Serenity opened the box and inhaled as deep as she could, then she put the lid back on and placed it in the BOM. Dawayne thought he saw a single tear trickle down her cheek, he wish she knew that this hurt him just as bad if not worse. He wanted her to be his Queen, his future baby mama, future wife. That moment had ended, he could no longer were his heart on his sleeve. Dawayne had to keep it covered with armor, he never wanted to feel that feeling again. Dawayne was at peace, and how he saw everything, how he saw the meaning of life. Clarity, Dawayne was thinking of Gravity by John Mayer. Got to stay grounded, he thought as he grabbed the orange and black duct tape to seal the BOM. He taped the box neatly and with a design or pattern.

He gave Serenity the tape once he was done, Serenity gave him the look. Then she ran to her room, Dawayne at first thought that she was going to cry into her pillow, she came back out with a bottle of cologne. It was the cologne he used when they first started talking, she sat it on the counter top. Dawayne shook his head, grabbed the bottle slowly. He placed it on the side of the box, and started taping it to the outside of the box. "You can't do that it will break," Serenity said. Dawayne looked at her, "if you think I'm going to open this package up to put that almost empty bottle in this damn box. That's not going to happen, sorry!" He finished taping the box, and then picked it up. He took it to his bedroom and placed it in the back corner of his closet, somewhere it wouldn't take a lot of space.

CLASS IS IN SESSION

(Extra Credit Needed)

Dawayne loaded a bowl and walked into the bathroom, Serenity followed in pursuit of Dawayne. The last thing Dawayne remembered doing was finding something to watch, and then he was pulling off Serenity's shirt. He almost ripped it with the sudden since of urgency that was running through his fuck muscle. Her shirt was over his head and then Dawayne used it to tie her hands above her head. He held on tight with his right arm, preventing her from moving her arms. He looked at her, looking beyond and connecting. He moved his head towards her ear, he slowly began to lick and whisper in her ear. He didn't even whisper any words, he just made a soft sound caused goosebumps to take over her body. His energy slowly flowed over her chilled body, warmth started to move from her feet. Serenity's giggled as he placed her toes in his mouth, given notice to each individual and then moving along the ankle. The warmth of his tongue felt as if it was thawing out an ice cube with only his breath. He moved to his favorite part the legs, long caramel canvas. Rolling and gliding of his tongue found their way between her thighs. "How many orgasms deed we get to that one night at the hotel? " Dawayne asked Serenity while talking to her vagina. "Like twelve, yeah twelve!" Dawayne lifted his head from between her thighs and said, "We're going to double that tonight and maybe a lil extra." He moved quickly to her chest her nipples were hard as fuck, his mouth moved along the milk chocolate nipple. Sucking on as much of her breast as he could switching from one to the other, making sure they each get the much attention they deserve. He moved to her neck and slowly began to suck, "Don't mark me." Serenity said, as he kept suckling on her neck. He was rough and gentle at the same time. Nibbling on her neck she moaned, his fingers tip toed to the warmth and very wet spot between her legs. One finger was able to slide in slowly, he began to move his finger as if he was. Slowly filling that lil hidden balloon with that nectar, he took his time slowly messaging the balloon with the tip of his finger. His mouth never left her body, he still kissed and sucked on any part he could reach. As his tongue moved liked fluid to her inner thigh, spelling one with his tongue he moved his tongue between her folds. Creating choreography with his tongue on her clit that was just slightly hidden. He moved the finger that was causing her to soon erupt, with speed and purpose he was going to make her squirt first orgasm. His finger hitting her spot like a Money Mayweather on a speed bag.

She cried out to the complex anybody that would listen that it felt good as fuck. Serenity looked into Dawayne's eyes, he looked at her. "I want you to let it rain on my, squirt me in the fucking face!" Keeping his finger moving at a steady pace, he positioned his face ready. He stuck out his tongue and then it happened, serenity started to squirt. The warm wet nectar covered his face, and most his body and sheets. Serenity's body tightened up, as squirted for what seemed like forever. He moved up to her body, not forgetting to kiss spots on his way to her neck. Then her her her looked at her and said, "That's one, twenty-three, what like twenty-five more." He said as he moved his muscle close to her glistening sweetness. Dawayne took his time, more slow and seductive them usual. As if this was the last time that he was going to make love to Serenity, they switched positions and played their sex games. The room was full of sexual energy, they had connected as one and they had moved to the next level. In the sex game Dawayne was All-Madden, Serenity was no longer a Rookie with all the sessions and LEVELS they had achieved. There were things Serenity never felt until she fell in love with him, she had never squirted or had a screaming orgasm. Dawayne used the head of his muscle and rubbed it along the outside of her sweetness. Serenity couldn't take it anymore, "You're such a fucking tease." Serenity said, pleading for him to just give it to her. Dawayne took his time, he slid the head in. Only the head and she tried to pull him in closer, he resisted and pulled the head out and then the savage started took over his body. He took the head and rubbed it along her clit, slid inside her extremely juicy pussay."Tease you, now why would I do that? I'm just getting that pussy prepared for what's about to happen to it," Dawayne said as he could feel the temperature in the room rise. "Say you want that nigga dick," sweat started to form on the brow of his head and he took himself and with all the energy, all his love for her, and he gave Serenity what she wanted. The savage took full control of his body and it gave her that nigga dick, Serenity came in seconds. Screaming at the top of her lungs, and growling the savage was inside of her and it felt fucking amazing. Dawayne could see what was happening, he could feel everything, as if his whole body was a nerve ending naked and exposed. There was pressure coming from inside, it was warm and it was trying to force him out. As his muscle slid in and out, she was full in every way. Pulling himself out just enough to release the warm nectar from within.

It came in short squirts, each time his tip was almost out she would give a lil squirt. This continued for what seemed like minutes, to Serenity it felt like forever and she didn't want it to end." How many is that?" Dawayne whispered in her ear. "FFFFfive or sixxxxxxxxx," She said trying not to stutter as she began to slide closer to the edge of the bed. She wasn't trying to get away it was just where her body ended up, the fitted sheet slipped off the mattress. He lifted her legs and put them on draped them over his shoulders. "Do you want it all, you want it deep?" "FFFFuck yes," Serenity growled. "Give it to me deep, fuck yes!!" He pulled her in closer, her hips were now in the air, and her juicy tight round volleyball ass was being gripped with his hands. As he gave her what she wanted and more, he squeezed her ass. Kissing whatever part of her legs he could, he was looking into her eyes, looking into her soul. The soul of her beast, her sexual demon. She attempted to grab the pillow and cover her face," Get that shit out of here." Dawayne said, as he grabbed the pillow and tossed it across the room. "Let that shit out, don't you fucking hold back on me!" Dawayne said, as he flipped Serenity on her stomach. He grabbed the closest pillow and gently lifting Serenity he placed the pillow under her hips. Serenity tried to be victim and get away, "You can't run from the nigga dick." She tried and seconds later found herself hanging half way off the bed, she found herself coming, coming harder than ever. He was beating that pussy up, Serenity thought and her legs began to shake. "You going to tap out on me?" he said to Serenity. "No!!" "Fuck no!" as she growled even more. It seemed they would always find themselves in the same position with Serenity barley on the bed, but that pussy though. That pussy was so good, he didn't want to stop. He paused to give her time to let her crawl back onto the bed, and when she did he was on his back. "I want you to ride that dick!" Serenity was hesitant she had done it only few times and had to jump off of him because the feeling was so intense. She couldn't hang before, but she had something to prove to him, something to prove to herself. She climb on and slid herself right on him, "Oh shit, oh shit!" Serenity said as she sat high, slowly sliding her juicy wet pussy on down his shaft. Grabbing Serenity he gripped her hips, lifting his ass off the bed. Giving her all of him, filling her up with every movement he made with his hips. Then he wrapped his arms around her and he went Marshawn Lynch on that pussy. He was looking at her expressions on her face, she was almost speechless.

She was still able to muster out a few syllables and sounds, that wasn't good enough he wanted to make her pass out. He wanted to make her squirt till she could no longer squirt, dehydrated like a mother fucker. He looked at her and feel in love all over again, she was amazing. She wasn't going to tap out on him, not like this. "Reverse!" Dawayne whispered quietly into Serenity's ear. She acted like she didn't hear him, he could tell by look she gave him that she heard him. "Slide that ass around on that dick, so I can see that ass twerk." Serenity acted shy, she slowly slid around facing the door. Serenity grabbed his dick and stroked it, he knew she was stalling. Once she slid his dick inside her pussy, he could tell immediately that this reverse cow girl was going to be his favorite of all cow girls. Serenity twerked her ass on his dick, he could see the thick white creamy nectar coating glistening from her walls. She was wet as fuck, she already came, and he was going to make her never forget him and this moment. Serenity arched her back as if she was trying to lay on him, to rest, to catch her breath. Dawayne raised his ass of the bed, giving her all of him again. She switched that up real quick and bent over, pulling herself down holding on to his legs. There was a quick movement that Dawayne noticed, just a quick movement. She was going to orgasm soon, she was now grinding on his dick like a beast in the night. Quick hip thrust, she was working it like Rihanna. "Werk, werk, werk,"popped up in Dawayne's head. Serenity was putting Rihanna to shame, Serenity started saying something but it was only babbling, she couldn't speak. "Oh shit, I think we found THE position." Dawayne said and chuckled a lil bit, Serenity looked at him and said, "I don't know what you're talking about!" She knew what he was talking about, every time she said that as her answer. She heard him the first time, no need to repeat. She tried to get off but Dawayne switched her grip on his legs and held her hands against his legs. Dawayne was hitting the spot, and he was going for the TAPOUT. She couldn't help herself from grinding on him, "It feels so, so fucking well!" "Shit I'm going to come, I'm going to FUCKING COME!" Serenity belted out with all the air in her lungs, it wasn't much but he heard her. He kept his grip on her hands, to his amazement she was still hanging on. She was holding it in, "You got to come too." She said belted out, as if she had been holding her breath the whole damn time. She sped up her grind, sliding on that dick hoping a genie would come out. Dawayne was feeling it now, fuck she was switching it up on him.

She was going to make him come now, it was like a battle to so who could make who come next. Dawayne has still not had a release yet, but he was close if she kept working that pussy the way she was. Dawayne snapped out of it and realized that she was trying to reverse the role. He switched his hips manipulating her to move to his rhythm, she slid right into rhythm. Once again he was the Dom and she was going to come again, and it was going to happen now. The room started to warm up again, sweat beaded down the middle of Serenity's back. "God that's so fucking sexy, "Dawayne said as he traced the bead of sweat with his finger to the top of her crack, then he split his fingers. Placing a finger from each hand on the middle of her back, then he slowly moved his fingers to her hips and then to her inner thigh. His fingers tingled as the pranced around her hips, Serenity was almost there. Her pace sped, her moans loader and longer, "I'm going to, I'm going to," Serenity screamed out, she began to dig her nails into the back of his calves. Then she found the strength to break away from his hands she slid her hand out tapping quickly. Then she hopped her pussy right off his dick and ran to get her inhaler. He felt a lil trickle hit his stomach, her pussy was CREAMY as a mother fucker. "You fucking tapped out on me, I can't believe this shit." He snickered, knowing that he made her come and tap out within seconds of each other. Serenity walked back into the bedroom with the inhaler in one hand, "I'm hungry, let's get something to eat." Dawayne rolled up out of the bed, grabbing some sweats and a t-shirt. "So when did you stop counting?" Dawayne asked Serenity, "I stopped counting at like twenty, and that was a long time ago!" "Let's go," Dawayne said looking at Serenity like why you still naked and not dressed yet. They left the house and hit up the lil diner not too far from them. Dawayne parked the car, looking around noticing there were quite a bit of cars in the parking lot at four in the morning. Walking fast to the entrance Dawayne opened the door for Serenity, the lady in the front greeted them and had them follow her to a booth. Serenity ordered chicken strips and chips, and Dawayne ordered a sandwich. Serenity brought up the events that just occurred at the house. "How did we fucking for hours get started in the first place?" She asked, "I'm still trying to wrap my head around what just happened." Dawayne said slowly, "Do you think we will always have a connection, and this crazy sexual connection we share?" I have no idea, only time will tell."

Serenity asked for a box from the waitress, and Dawayne waited for the check to come back with his change. Their server came back with the change. Happy Valentine's Day, a woman said to them as they walked out the door. The both looked each other realizing they just fucked from last night, to mother fucking Valentine's Day. "Fucking Valentine's Day," they both said jumping into the car laughing. Dawayne cranked the tunes up and they headed back to the house.

HELLO MY NAME IS KARMA

I'm here to fuck YOUR day up, and LIFE if possible.

Karma, some people say that it's life
Bitch slapping you
In the face every now and then.
Life just has to
Let you know that your just a
Human on this earth.
It's also been said that Karma is the big decision
In your life
You wish you could take back,
Coming full circle just to show what could have been.
Karma has many faces
And wears them all well,
When things are going well
Karma is lurking in the shadows.
Don't forget this is true shit,
If Karma hasn't found you yet.
You soon will SEE

Dawayne and Serenity had an energetic and easy going relationship, they would fuck with each other all the time. Poor pitchers of cold water on each other as they would shower. Randomly eat the rest of their favorite snack, whatever it was they always kept increasing the intensity of the joke or prank. It had been a few months shroom night. It had also been a week or two since they has a sex session. While he was trying to bring their relationship to a mends, Serenity was given a decision to make, and she was deciding to LEAVE. There wasn't much of a choice to leave, both decisions had the ending result as leaving. Dawayne had been not feeling himself, hell the woman that made him whole was leaving for good. This was real and there was nothing he could do, he fought until his heart got the T.K.O.

Dawayne was in a good mood as he walked into the apartment, he could hear music in the bathroom and the shower running. The idea popped into his head, he laughed to himself. Thinking of his grand master plan to fuck with Serenity while she was in the shower. He thought of taking her towel, only thing she did that to him so many times he needed something different. He could turn the light off on her, he chuckled and hit the switch, and he waited for a scream or the fuck. Time started ticking fast, there was no sound no, nothing. He click the switch back on and went to the bathroom. Serenity was in the corner of the shower freaking the fuck out. She was crying and freaking out on him, "What the fuck were you doing, you know I'm scared of the dark." It hit Dawayne with an automatic sickening feeling in his gut, he fucked up. He fucked up because he wasn't thinking, yea living in the moment was a good motto to live by. Consequences of living in the moment can't be made by not completely thinking of what may happen. How big of an impact will this make, Dawayne knew after that that two strikes he was out. After that afternoon, their chemistry was off. The minutes turned into hours and the days to weeks, the day had been, marked on the calendar. Serenity rolled out of bed and went into the kitchen, Dawayne was getting his keys off the counter. He turned to see Serenity, he pulled her in and wrapped his arms around her. She wrapped her arms around him as tight as she could. Not wanting to let go, he knew this could be an END. As his fingertips touched her finger tips, what particles that held them TOGETHER evaporated. As he turned his back he had to hold back tears, although one sneaked its way to the tip of his nose.

He may NEVER see her again, the FINAL chapter to a great MOMENT. The summer to end all SUMMERS. Is this a summer thing or an every summer thing? The lyrics grooved through his frontal lobe and pin balled from lobe to lobe. Until it reached his cerebellum, Dawayne chuckled shutting the door behind him. He headed down to his car and from there the autobahn, his Bluetooth was playing songs from their playlist. He switched to a cd already set to play, that wasn't any better, then the radio. He heard Whitney's voice, he closed his eyes for a brief moment. Consciencly saying fuck you, and with one last breath he said, "KARMA IS A BITCH!"

SHOUT OUTS

My lil sis T
You told me to run with it and now look. Ci
Without you the story would exist

Dave
You told me I needed a chapter to let the reader know
more about me.... You told me Origins of a Sexual
Savage

Riah
You know!!!!

My Madre
For being the dopest mother, you have been nothing but
supportive.

My BLINK FAM
Some of you read it when it was only a chapter, and
others heard about it so were skur'd lmbao. It's all good.

Lisha
What are neighbors good for? To read what you have
and tell you if you have a good story or not..

Last but not LEAST and biggest help during this adventure...

MUSIC
My first book has a play-list, look back and find them.
Music is always a good book mark in life and for me
these songs brought back memories. Music is Medicine

"Surround yourself with good people, and good vibes"

Printed in the United States
By Bookmasters